SEEING RED

By the time we got on our feet and had our bearings, the pooch was halfway up the stairs. We chased after the beast—it was a wide stairs and we were able to climb side by side. I may have a decade on Susannah, but she had her clothes to contend with. Frankly, however, neither of us is fit. We huffed and puffed our way across a marble landing and were halfway up the second set when we both noticed the blood. It was dark, more black than red, and stood out sharply on the pale gray marble.

I looked up. At the head of the stairs was an arm, bent backward, and the top of someone's head. The hair was naturally red. "Don't look," I said. We both stared. I knew without getting any closer that it was certainly a corpse. I've been around death enough to know that it has its own peculiar smell. . . .

THE HAND THAT ROCKS THE LADLE

A PENNSYLVANIA DUTCH MYSTERY WITH RECIPES

Tamar Myers

A SIGNET BOOK

SIGNET
Published by New American Library, a division of
Penguin Putnam Inc., 375 Hudson Street,
New York, New York 10014, U.S.A.
Penguin Books Ltd, 27 Wrights Lane,
London W8 5TZ, England
Penguin Books Australia Ltd, Ringwood,
Victoria, Australia
Penguin Books Canada Ltd, 10 Alcorn Avenue,
Toronto, Ontario, Canada M4V 3B2
Penguin Books (N.Z.) Ltd, 182–190 Wairau Road,
Auckland 10, New Zealand

Penguin Books Ltd, Registered Offices:
Harmondsworth, Middlesex, England

First published by Signet, an imprint of New American Library,
a division of Penguin Putnam Inc.

First Printing, March 2000
10 9 8 7 6 5 4 3 2 1

Ⓢ REGISTERED TRADEMARK—MARCA REGISTRADA

Printed in the United States of America

PUBLISHER'S NOTE
This is a work of fiction. Names, characters, places, and incidents either are
the product of the author's imagination or are used fictitiously, and any resemblance to actual persons, living or dead, business establishments, events, or
locales is entirely coincidental.

For my sisters:

Carolyn Yost
Marilyn Memmer
Evelyn Moler

One

Amish men rarely get pregnant. Elderly Amish men almost never do. Mose Hostetler, however, seemed to be the exception.

When Freni first told me the news, I had to stifle my impulse to laugh. "What do you mean Mose is going to have a baby?"

"Not just one baby, Magdalena, but *three.* My Mose is going to have triplets."

"Freni, dear," I said gently, "it's your daughter-in-law, Barbara, who is going to have triplets. Mose is going to have a nice long vacation."

Freni Hostetler, Mose's wife, flapped her arms like a rooster about to crow. "Yah, Barbara is having triplets, but so is my Mose. I could feel the babies—all three of them."

"Where?"

She clutched her own apron-clad abdomen. "Here. I could feel them kick."

I rolled my eyes and prayed for patience. I also promised myself I wouldn't worry needlessly about my cook and her husband.

That was three months ago, and my eyes had put on more miles than a roller derby. As for the patience, it never did come. How can one be patient with a seventy-three-year-old man who claims to have morning sickness? All that talk about hemorrhoids and constipation was enough to put me off my feed. I must have lost ten pounds, while the grandfather-to-be gained twenty. Thank heavens Amish law forbids men to dress in women's clothes; Mose in a maternity smock is a sight these eyes never want to see. And of course I worried.

I couldn't help worrying about Freni and Mose. Ever since my parents' tragic death eleven years ago in a tunnel—squished between a milk tanker and a semi loaded to the gills with state-of-the-art running shoes—the two have been like parents to me. Who knows, by some strange genetic quirk, they might even *be* my parents. You see, the Hostetlers are Amish, and I am a Mennonite of Amish descent. Our families have been intermarrying for hundreds of years. Mose and Freni are distant cousins to each other, as well as to me. It would take a professional genealogist to sort out our exact relationships. Suffice it to say, our bloodlines are so tangled that I am, in fact, my own cousin. If I'm in the mood for a family picnic, all I need to do is make a sandwich.

But a body can do only so much worrying, and as the months dragged by, I threw myself into my work like never before. I am the owner and proprietress of the PennDutch Inn in the sleepy little hamlet of Hernia, Pennsylvania. It has been said, by others than myself, that mine is the finest full-board inn west of the Alleghenies. I like to think that is because of my personal touch, and because of A.L.P.O.

"A.L.P.O.," I said to my new guest, "stands for Amish Lifestyle Plan Option. For an extra twenty dollars a day I'll let you make your own bed and clean your own room. For an extra thirty dollars you get to help in the kitchen."

The guest stared at me from beneath eyebrows the size of feather dusters. For the record, I have never seen eyes that pale. They were gray, but so thinly pigmented that a myriad of veins showed through, causing the impression of pink.

"Surely you jest," he said.

"Not at all. It says here on your registration form that you're here to study the Amish. What better way than to immerse yourself in their way of life."

"What better way for you to enrich your coffer."

Coffer? I glanced at the form again. Ah, yes, the man was a professor of sociology. That would explain the somewhat shabby suit, the snagged polyester tie, and the extravagant vocabulary.

I sighed. There is no point in trying to fleece an academic—not that I would try to do such a thing mind you. I am a good Christian woman, after all. What I mean is, in my experience, educators tend to be as tightfisted as dead boxers. Of course it is because they are underpaid. I understand that. Still, I would be lucky if I didn't end up owing *him* at the end of his stay.

"Mr. Barnes, your room—"

"That's Doctor."

"I beg your pardon?"

"My title is Dr. Barnes. Don't you see the Ph.D. after my name?"

"Of course I see it," I said pleasantly. "What about it?"

Watery eyes regarded me unwaveringly. "I must insist that you address me as Dr. Barnes."

I smiled. "I must insist that you address me as Proprietress."

"That's preposterous."

"Tit for tat," I said calmly. "I won't stand on ceremony if you won't."

Feather-duster eyebrows converged into one enormous thicket. "Just show me to my room, Proprietress."

I led him up the impossibly steep stairs to the guest rooms. (Yes, I do have an elevator, but why waste electricity?) If pressed, I will admit that for one split second I had the wicked urge to give him a slight push backward with the heel of my foot. Of course I wouldn't really do such a thing. A woman guest already met her demise at the base of those stairs, and let me tell you this, there is nothing that can be done about a dent in a hardwood floor.

But I digress. The point is, my guest lineup for that first week of October had not gotten off to a good start. And either I was coming down with a touch of arthritis, or I could feel trouble in my bones. It was not going to be a good week.

TWO

Perhaps I should introduce myself. My full name is Magdalena Portulaca Yoder. I stand five feet ten in my bare feet, have been accused of being thin, and have a negative chest profile. I have a large head, and unkind people have suggested that my elongated proboscis would make a good cheese-cutting implement. As stated before, I am an orphan—albeit a middle-aged orphan. I have one sister, Susannah Yoder Entwhistle Stoltzfus, and since I don't count the miniature dog she carries around in her bra as blood kin, I have no nephews (a fact she disputes). I would describe myself as fair-minded and reasonably tolerant of other folks' proclivities.

Thank heavens, however, my next two guests were as down to earth as plowshares. Hailing from Indiana, the Redigers were perhaps in their mid-thirties, and the epitome of wholesomeness. Neither had any extraneous initials attached to their name, and they listed their occupations as carpenter and housewife respectively. Donald was clean-cut, neatly dressed in khaki slacks and blue, long-sleeved chambray shirt. Gloria wore a dress that properly covered her knees. Her brown braids were swept back and piled in a bun.

"Ah, fellow Mennonites," I said, unable to suppress a smile.

The Redigers smiled back. "We've come east to see the fall color," Donald said.

"But there doesn't seem to be much," Gloria said. It was a simple statement of fact, not a complaint.

I shook my oversized noggin. "I'm sorry, folks, but we've had a dry summer and, well, to tell you the truth, you're about ten days too early. Mid-October though, the mountainsides should be a blaze of color. I don't suppose you'd care to stay until then."

Gloria shook her plain, but pretty head. Although she lacked a prayer cap—many modern Mennonites go without these days—the thick brown braids, gathered in back and held neatly in place with a myriad of simple hairpins, were a dead giveaway that she was of my faith.

"I'm afraid a week is all we can afford," she said softly. Her Hoosier accent was barely noticeable.

I thought fast. I really didn't need the money. My inn has done very well over the years, and despite a president with zipper problems, the economy has been good to me as well.

"Tell you what, dears, I just happen to have a special plan called A.L.P.O.—Amish Liberals Partly Off. That's you. You're Mennonites, which is sort of like being liberal Amish, so you get partly off. Provided you clean your own rooms, of course."

The Redigers exchanged anxious glances. "Is that legal?" Donald asked.

"Well—"

"How much off?" Gloria asked.

I strode casually from behind the check-in counter and peeked surreptitiously at her shoes. They were obviously not genuine leather, and had seen much better days.

"Half off. That way you can stay the whole two weeks for the price of one."

The Redigers beamed, which in turn brought a smile to my face. I really do like it when my guests are happy. As to any accusations that I had just shown partiality—well, I did. And so be it. We all show partiality at some time or another. Anyone who disagrees with that is not being totally honest, and to me that's a lot worse sin than showing favoritism. Even the Good Lord had a favorite disciple, for crying out loud.

"God bless you," Donald cried.

"You are so kind," Gloria said. "Half off! It is truly an answer to prayer."

I put a slender finger to my lips. "Shhh. The English will hear you."

By that I meant the pompous professor. The Amish, and some of the stricter Mennonites, refer to those outside the tradition as English. It is an appellation that has nothing to do with origin. Indeed, the Japanese are every bit as English to the Amish as are Londoners. In other words, English is our word for *goyim*.

The Redigers knew exactly what I meant. They nodded their heads, and Gloria giggled nervously. I felt almost ebullient. It had been a long time since I'd had Mennonite guests—okay, to be truthful, these were my first Mennonite guests. Please understand, however, that we Mennonites are a simple people and not given to gallivanting needlessly around the country. At any rate, the ache in my bones that commenced with Professor Barnes's appearance was gone. Things were looking up again.

* * *

No sooner had I shown the grateful Redigers to their rooms when two *real* English guests showed up. Daphne and Edwina Moregold had written ahead from their home in Manchester, England, so they were expected. And since I have had real English guests before, I expected there would be some difficulty in communication (I shall hereby translate everything the Moregold sisters said for your edification). What I didn't expect was a pair of identical twins.

"Which one is which?" I asked gamely.

The women, incidentally, appeared to be in their late fifties, early sixties. But given the English reputation for youthful, dewy complexions, and the fact that both were overweight, they might well have been a lot older.

"I'm Edwina, the eldest," one of the plump, pink-cheeked sisters said.

"I'm Daphne, the youngest," the other said.

"Fat lot of good that does," I wailed, and then mentally slapped myself for having used the F word in front of them.

"I've got the beauty mark here. See?" Edwina, I think, pushed a lock of graying hair away from her convex forehead. A microscopic mole greeted my myopic eyes.

"She's far too proud of that thing if you ask me," her sister said.

I smiled pleasantly. "Then maybe she should display it."

"All right." Edwina fished a rubber band (what the folks in Pittsburgh call a gum band) out of her purse, and pulled her shoulder-length hair back into a short, but revealing ponytail.

What a difference a hairstyle makes. The two peas in a pod were now more like a bean and a pea. Sure, their bone structure remained the same, but now Daphne's individual personality was on display along with her beauty mark.

"Ah, that's much better," I said. "Now, if I recall correctly, you wrote to the Pennsylvania Tourist Bureau for accommodations in Amish country, and they sent you two a brochure. Have you two made up your minds yet about the A.L.P.O plan?"

"We definitely want it," Edwina said. "We wish to absorb as much American culture as possible."

"We're thinking of retiring here," Daphne explained.

"Oh?"

"Of course that won't be for another thirty years, but it never hurts to plan ahead."

"At least thirty years," Edwina said.

I glanced down at the registration form. Call me nosy if you will, but I ask for more information than do other hostelries. At any rate, the twins were only *twenty-nine*. They both worked as machinists, making industrial-size bobbins for textile factories. Much to my surprise, I felt sorry for them.

"The brochure contained several misprints," I said. While lying is a sin, I'm quite sure some lies are not as bad as others. "You see, the brochure stated that guests would have to pay an extra twenty dollars a day for the privilege of cleaning their own rooms. What I meant to say is that I would deduct twenty dollars."

Edwina cleared her throat. "Is that twenty dollars off *per* day?"

"Yes," I heard these lips say.

Two sets of identical green eyes sparkled. Daphne actually clapped her hands.

"What lovely news," she said. "Now we shall be able to see more of your wonderful country."

"Is it far to Disney World?" Edwina asked. She had pulled a pocket atlas from a purse and was thumbing through it. I saw Idaho and New Mexico flip by.

I knew that the women had flown directly from London to Pittsburgh, where they'd rented a car. It takes me two hours to get to the Pittsburgh International Airport from Hernia, and I've been accused of having heavy feet—not lead feet, mind, just heavy feet. It seems to go with size eleven.

"Did you think it was far from Pittsburgh?" I asked.

They nodded vigorously in tandem, as if sharing only one short neck. "I remarked to Daphne that it was like driving halfway across England."

"Farther," Daphne said. "Is Pennsylvania the largest state?"

I smiled. "I've heard rumors that Texas is larger. As for Disney World, it's fifteen times farther than Pittsburgh. You may want to fly."

The sisters looked crestfallen. "I'm afraid we can't afford to," Edwina said quietly.

I skirted the counter once again and studied their shoes. Both pairs were sturdy leather, well polished, but obviously very old.

"Okay, you can have the room at half price and I'll help you look for a supersaver."

They looked blank.

"A cheap flight," I said.

Daphne brushed a stray wisp away from her beauty mark. "Are the hotels at Disney World expensive?"

I gave them a pitying look. "Okay, scratch the

A.L.P.O. I won't charge you anything while you're here."

They gasped simultaneously.

"You mean we can stay for free?" Edwina said.

I grimaced. "*Please,* dear, nothing in this world is ever really free. To the contrary. You will set and clear tables, wash dishes, and muck out the barn."

"The *barn*?" they chorused.

I nodded. "I have a seventy-three-year-old pregnant Amish man doing it as we speak, but he really isn't up to the task."

Both sets of green eyes blinked.

"It's a long story, dears. Say, can either of you milk a cow?"

They grinned. "Our granddad has a farm in Devonshire."

"Well, I just happen to have two cows who need milking on a twice daily basis. Their names are Matilda and Bessie."

"Super," Edwina said. "Daphne here makes the best Devonshire cream—although it wouldn't be proper Devonshire cream here, would it? Still, if clotted cream is what you're after, Daphne is your woman."

Daphne beamed.

"What is clotted cream?" I had the coarseness to ask.

"Ah, that's what rises to the top when you scald milk. It's thicker, sweeter, and richer than whipped cream, and is delicious atop scones with jam." She pronounced scones to rhyme with johns.

"Do you make scones as well?" I asked, drooling only slightly.

Daphne shook her head. "Edwina is the baker. Scones, tarts, you name it."

"I'd be happy to bake some for you, if Daphne will make her cream."

"It would be my pleasure," Daphne said. "We could have a proper cream tea."

I hustled the twins up to their rooms before I got really carried away and offered them a salary.

I am not easily shocked, having played hostess to half of Hollywood during my inn's heyday. Trust me, there are those in that crowd who know no shame. One ingenue even bragged to me about breaking all ten of the commandments at once—only not in my inn, thank heavens. Still, before she checked out, I inspected her room for corpses and counted my best flatware. At any rate, I wasn't so much shocked, but appalled, by my next two guests.

She was tall and thin, approximately my age, but unlike me as brown as a hickory nut. Her color was related to her minority status which, incidentally, had nothing to do with race, but everything to do with a leisurely life in the sun. Vivian Mays was what my mama would have called "stinking rich." It was a wonder she could even hold her head up, given the size and weight of the gold chains she wore draped around her neck.

He was also well tanned, although dark eyebrows and dark roots betrayed the pale blond hair on his head. He too wore jewelry, most notably an earring. Alas, it wasn't a simple gold hoop, which I wouldn't have found too objectionable, but a pearl that dangled from a little platinum chain. Oh, well, kids these days.

From what I hear, it's the rare parent who can exercise control.

"You didn't say you were bringing your son with you," I said through gritted teeth. I had two more guest rooms available, but hadn't bothered to make them up.

"He *isn't* my son," she said through capped, but gritted teeth.

I raised an eyebrow. "Your grandson?"

"My *husband!*"

I stared at the boy. He couldn't have been a day over eighteen. And she—add ten years for sun exposure, take off ten for plastic surgery—she *had* to be my age.

"You're putting me on!"

"I most certainly am not. It says so right there on that form you just made us fill out."

I stared at the form. The boy was just barely twenty, and she was nine days *older* than I! I had to prop myself against the counter for support.

"But you didn't say you were married when you called and made reservations," I wailed. "In fact, you said you were a widow."

Vivian looked at my ring finger, and then smiled like the cat who had licked the clotted cream dish. "I am—*was* a widow. And I didn't say anything about Sandy because I didn't know him then."

"But that was less than a month ago!"

"I guess I'm just a lucky woman. I mean, what else can I say?"

Fortunately Freni came running into the room, her stubby arms flailing like the blades of a broken windmill. "Help! Help!"

"Freni, what is it? You see your reflection in aluminum foil again?"

"Ach, no! It's Mose!"

My heart did a flip-flop. "He wasn't up on the barn roof again, was he?"

"Ach no, it's much more serious than that. His water broke."

Three

"You mean he peed in his pants, don't you?" I
avoided looking at the rich woman and her
child groom.

"Yah, but you know what that means, Magdalena?"

"It means you need to take him home and get his
clothes changed."

"Ach, so dense! It means that my Barbara has gone
into labor."

"Your *daughter-in-law,*" I said for the benefit of our
audience, "lives on your farm which is more than a
mile away. You don't have a phone, and anyway, my
phone didn't ring. How do you know Barbara's in
labor? What did she do, send up smoke signals?"

Freni rolled her eyes. "A *mother* knows these
things."

My cheeks burned. I am not a mother, nor will I
ever be. I had a sham marriage to a bigamist that
lasted exactly one month, and although he created
enough opportunities to populate a small third world
nation, I did not conceive. Of course I know now that
it was the Good Lord's doing, and that Aaron Miller
was the devil incarnate and utterly unfit to be a father.
But let's face it, even if I were to marry tomorrow, I
doubt I would ever hear the pitter-patter of tiny

human feet. The minute hand on my biological clock
has stopped ticking. As for adoption, the agency I approached told me in no uncertain terms that there had
to be "at least one stable adult in the household."

At any rate, don't believe for a minute that Freni
had me stumped. I still would have thought of some
pithy rejoinder had not her son Jonathan Hostetler
come flapping through the front door, a giant version
of his mother.

"Ach!" he squawked. "Come quick! My Barbara is
broken and her water is having triplets!"

Freni gave me an "I told you so" look. "You will
drive us to the hospital, yah?"

"Yah, yah," I said irritably. "Where is the mother
to be?"

Jonathan's eyes were wild. "Outside in my buggy.
Come, we have no time to talk."

Vivian the vamp and her sex slave Sandy had been
watching the proceedings mutely. Thank the Good
Lord for that. But all the commotion had attracted
that delightful Mennonite couple, Donald and Gloria
Rediger.

"Miss Yoder," Gloria said kindly, "is there anything
we can do?"

"Yes! Call the hospital and tell them we're coming.
Then call Dr. Pierce's office—his practice is in Bedford. The numbers are posted by the kitchen phone."

"Anything else?"

I slapped my forehead with the palm of my right
hand. "There's a wet Amish man in the barn. Get him
some dry clothes and bring him to the hospital. It's
just south of town. You take Hertzler Road to Main
Street and—oh, never mind, he knows the way."

"We'll take care of him," Donald said, and not even

knowing which direction the barn was, they rushed off to help.

"Here is your room key!" I slapped a six-inch piece of wood with an attached key into Vivian's manicured hand. "That's a new bed in Room Five. You break it, you buy it."

I turned my attention to my kinsfolk. "I'll move my car around to the front. Freni, get a plastic tablecloth to spread in the backseat. Jonathan, unhitch your horse and get ready to transfer Barbara." And then, just for fun, I hollered up my impossibly steep stairs. "Somebody boil water!"

Thank heavens Hernia finally has its own hospital. A town our size would never be able to support one if it wasn't for the hundreds of Amish and Mennonite families who prefer to avoid the streets of Babylon— I mean Bedford. Granted, ours is a very small facility, more suited to emergency care than anything else, but it is handy. Fortunately I had yet to use it, but I had heard only good things about it.

We arrived at the hospital in the nick of time. Just a few minutes later and baby number one would have been born in the backseat of my BMW, and not on the gurney. As it was, I was going to have to get my car detailed at the earliest possible opportunity.

At any rate, a young orderly named Gordon helped Jonathan and me transfer Barbara to the gurney, and then we took off running for the front door. Just as we passed the admissions counter a giant hand reached down and grabbed me by the collar of my navy blue dress. For one panicky second I thought God was calling me up yonder. I am ready, by the way, so don't get me wrong; it's just that my underwear had holes in them.

"Oh, no, you don't!" Although the voice was female, I knew it wasn't God because of the Pittsburgh accent.

I turned my head the best I could. "Nurse Dudley?"

"Yeah, what about it?"

In the meantime Jonathan and Freni had disappeared along with the gurney through a set of swinging double doors.

"Unhand me at once!"

The bruiser practically threw me across the small waiting room. "Get out of my hospital, Magdalena Yoder."

I gasped. "This is not your hospital! You work at Bedford Community Hospital along with the evil Dr. Luther."

Nurse Dudley, a behemoth of a woman with a neck as big around as a dinner plate, smiled. "This is my hospital now. I'm the R.N. supervisor."

I must have blanched. I certainly felt weak in the knees.

"What's the matter, Magdalena? Don't you read the papers?"

No doubt by now you've assumed that Nurse Dudley and I have had our run-ins before. If that's the case, you are absolutely right. The woman is—how can I put this the most Christian way possible? The woman is a cretin. She has the IQ of concrete and the personality of a cobra.

"Of course I read the papers!" I cried. I do. I read Ann Landers, the comics page, and if I have time, the editorial page.

"Then you'd know that not only am I the head

nurse, but the *evil* Dr. Luther—as you put it—is the chief of staff."

My head spun. The only thing that kept me from fainting was my fear that the diabolical duo would do something horrible to me while I was out. Like amputate my larynx.

"Well, the two of you might have somehow wormed your way past the board of directors and hospital administrator, but you don't *own* the place."

The battle-ax took a step closer. Her neck was now the size of a washtub.

"That might be, Yoder, but none of them are here right now. I, however, am."

"You lay a hand on me again and I'll sue!" I wailed. "I know both Johnny Cochran and Marcia Clark."

"I bet you do."

"But I *do*! They've stayed at my inn. I even know Kenneth Starr!"

That seemed to make an impression on her, because she took two steps back. I dodged around her, but the second I reached the set of swinging doors, they swung open and I ran smack into Freni. Fortunately for both of us she is well padded.

"Ach!"

"Sorry! What are you doing coming back out? Where's Jonathan? Where's *Barbara*?"

"They went into the delivery room." Her chin quivered. "They won't let me in!"

"Then come, sit with me." I dragged her back into the waiting room, and under the dour gaze of Nurse Dudley, held her hand while we waited. And waited, and *waited*. And while we waited, I worried. The Redigers had yet to show up with Mose. What if they'd taken a wrong turn and were headed south toward

Maryland? I'd been weaned on tales of folks who'd crossed that line, never to return.

Finally I could stand the wait no longer. I hoofed it over to the admissions desk.

"I need to use the phone."

"It's for staff use only."

"Then where's the public phone?"

Nurse Dudley smiled sadistically. "It's outside, but I'm afraid it's out of order."

"Then can you at least tell me what's happening in the delivery room?"

"No can do."

I pointed to Freni. "But that's her son and daughter-in-law in there! Those are her grandbabies! What am I supposed to tell her?"

"Tell her to keep waiting. This is, after all, a waiting room."

"Well, we'll just see about that!" I strode back to Freni, grabbed one of her tiny hands, and pulled her through the swinging doors.

Alas, we had barely set foot in the hallway when a second set of double doors swung open and there, coming straight at me, was Dr. Luther. I gasped. He growled.

"You!" he said, wagging a finger at me in a presidential manner. "What are you doing back here?"

I stood my ground. Under normal circumstances—say, if I'd met the man at church—I would think him a very handsome man. My sister Susannah says he looks like Clark Kent. I do not watch television, but I will say this: there have been a couple of times when I've dreamed of Luther and woken up feeling very guilty. But don't get me wrong. He's a mean and spiteful man. Malicious even. He once had me thrown out of Bedford Community Hospital.

"Where are the Hostetlers?" I demanded.

"That's none of your business, Yoder." He pronounced my name to rhyme with otter, which is *not* how one should pronounce it.

"But it's her business!" I pointed at Freni who was ringing her stubby hands. "Those are her grandbabies being born."

The evil man glowered at me over horn-rimmed glasses. "Get out of my hospital before I call the police!"

"Call. See if I care. For your information, buster, the chief of police here is my brother-in-law."

Alas, those words are true. Melvin Stoltzfus is married to my sister, Susannah. The man—and I say this in all kindness—is a twit. He once sent his favorite aunt a carton of ice cream in the *mail*.

Dr. Luther had the audacity to laugh. "Yes, I know he's your brother-in-law. And from what I hear, the two of you can't stand each other."

"Yes, well, Melvin's mother, Elvina, is Freni's best friend."

"Is that so? Well, in that case, I'll make an exception for you, Mrs. Hostetler. In fact, I'll personally escort you back to the delivery room." He glowered at me again. "You, however—out!"

Benedict Freni beamed.

I, of course, was properly outraged. "Why I never! If Dr. Gabriel Rosen were in charge—"

Freni pinched my elbow. "Shush, Magdalena. He doesn't want to hear about your new boyfriend, and I want to see my babies."

"Your *grand*babies, dear," I reminded her. "They're Barbara's babies."

"What did you say?" Dr. Luther demanded.

"I said, they're not her babies. As far as Freni is concerned, Barbara is just a handy conveyance for Little Freni and her siblings."

"Ach!"

"No, Yoder, before that. What did you say about Dr. Gabriel Rosen?"

"*I* said that." Freni would wave for attention in a police lineup.

"Yes?"

My plump, elderly kinswoman not only smiled coyly at the evil physician, she went so far as to link her arm through his. "I said you didn't want to hear about her new boyfriend. So now we go back and see my babies, yah?"

Dr. Luther shook Freni's arm loose like a flake of dry snow. "This wouldn't happen to be *the* Dr. Gabriel Rosen, the famous heart surgeon would it? I mean, I'd heard rumors that he had retired and moved to somewhere in this part of the state. I just thought they were too good to be true."

"Heart-shmart," Freni humphed. "If God would have wanted us to transplant hearts he would have put zippers in our chests."

"You don't even believe in zippers," I hissed. "And yes, Doc, he's the one. Like I was about to say, if he were in charge of this rinky-dink hospital, we'd be back there right now watching my little namesake being born."

"Ach!"

Dr. Luther actually smiled at me. It was the first,

and hopefully last time. Some folks really do look better grim.

"I don't suppose you'd be willing to make an introduction would you, Miss Yoder?" His pronunciation of my name had now changed. "You see, it is my dream to someday add a cardiac care unit here. Maybe—just maybe, he would be willing to consult with us."

"*Maybe,*" I said, "but not likely, considering the way you've treated me over the years."

Dr. Luther turned the color of Freni's pickled beets. "You have my deepest apology, Miss Yoder. I don't know what I was thinking."

"You were thinking that I was a meddlesome nobody."

His color turned even deeper. "I would like to make that up to you. Come"—he actually grabbed my arm—"we'll put you in scrubs and you can watch your little namesake come into this world."

"Ach!" Freni had latched on to me with a hand that only death could open. "Where she goes, I go, and the first little girl to be born will be named Freni, *not* Magdalena."

The swinging doors flew open and in stumbled seventy-three-year-old Mose. Hot on his heels was the diabolical Dudley.

"He wouldn't stay in a wheelchair," she barked.

"Ach, I'm not sick! I'm having babies."

I rolled my eyes in embarrassment. I was, however, immensely relieved.

The loathsome Luther loosened his grip on my arm. "What did you say?"

Nurse Dudley laughed like a hyena on steroids. "He thinks he's pregnant."

Mose clutched his abdomen and groaned.

Dr. Luther nodded. "I get it now. You," he said to Mose, "are my *present* from the staff of Bedford Community Hospital. Right? Their sick idea of a practical joke. What insensitive, politically incorrect name do you call yourself? A rental mental?"

Freni flapped her arms in alarm. "Ach, he's just my husband."

"It's a sympathetic pregnancy," I explained. "Although I must admit, he's taking it too far. Labor pains, indeed."

"But it's true!" Freni wailed. "I felt the babies kick."

Nurse Dudley pointed to her own head, and with a finger almost as thick as my wrists made a circular motion. "She's just as crazy as he is."

"Maybe he's really sick," I snapped. "Maybe he has appendicitis."

"Don't be ridiculous—"

Dr. Luther had put up a quieting hand. "Where exactly does it hurt, Mr. Hostetler?"

Mose pointed to the lower right quarter of his abdomen. "Here," he moaned.

The doctor leaned forward, and using the first two fingers of his right hand, gently palpated Mose's belly. "Hmm," he said at last, "there might be something to this appendix theory."

Nurse Dudley glared at me. "Just you wait," she whispered.

Dr. Luther straightened. "Nurse, get this man into an examining room."

The battle-ax didn't budge. "You're not falling for their little trick, are you?"

"Nurse!" Dr. Luther's stock soared in my eyes.

"But—"

"Mama! Papa!"

Five heads swiveled to look down the hall to the second set of swinging doors. Jonathan Hostetler, still dressed in scrubs, was lurching toward us, a lopsided grin on his face.

Freni paled. "Ach! My babies! Are they all right?"

Jonathan lurched close enough to give his mother a hug, but like me, he was genetically incapable of unnecessary human contact. He looked radiant nonetheless.

"Little Jonathan and Little Mose are doing fine."

"And?" Freni coaxed.

"And Barbara too."

"Ach, that's not who I mean! How is Little Freni?"

Jonathan shook his head. "Sorry, Mama, but there is no Little Freni."

Freni gasped, momentarily depleting the hallway of oxygen. "What"—she struggled to say—"what do you mean there is no Little Freni."

"He means," I said gently, "that the third child is a boy."

Tears filled Jonathan's blue eyes, and his lower lip quivered. "No! There is no third child."

Four

I smiled reassuringly at Freni. "Don't tease your mama like that, Jonathan. Of course there is a third baby. I drove Barbara into Bedford for all her checkups."

Jonathan blinked. "Yah, but still, there are only two babies."

Freni was as white as her homemade cottage cheese. "Are you sure?" she asked, lapsing into her native Pennsylvania Dutch.

"Yah, very sure."

I whirled to face Nurse Dudley. "Get Dr. Pierce!"

Nurse Dudley recoiled in shock.

"Go on and get him. He'll tell you he heard three heartbeats. He'll tell you he saw three tiny people on the ultrasound screen."

"Dr. Pierce," she said fiercely, "isn't here."

"*What?* I told Gloria Rediger to call him."

Dr. Luther folded his hands, and then opened them, fingertips touching to form a tent. He cleared his throat, adjusted his horn-rimmed glasses, and cleared his throat again.

"I'm afraid Dr. Pierce is not associated with this hospital."

"What does that mean?"

"Yah," Freni wailed, "explain!"

Dr. Luther started to smile, and then wisely abandoned the idea. "It means that since we are a small hospital, many of the Bedford physicians can't be bothered to affiliate. Dr. Pierce was one of them. He did, however, refer a number of his local patients to our staff obstetrician, Dr. Bauer. It was he who delivered the Hostetler infants."

"Then get him!" I shouted.

"Magdalena, please," Jonathan said, "there is no need. I was there. Just two babies—that's all I saw."

"Gut Himmel!" Mose groaned and collapsed on the floor at our feet.

Freni shrieked, Jonathan shouted, and I may have added to the din as well. While the three of us vocalized, the burly nurse and evil Luther carried Mose, like a sack of potatoes, into the nearest examining room. We tried to follow, but with one swift kick, Nurse Dudley was able to slam the door in our faces. And though I don't recall ever seeing them at other hospitals, *this* hospital had locks on the doors.

"Ach, my Mose," Freni wailed piteously, "what will I do without him?"

Jonathan prevailed over centuries of inbreeding long enough to put a clumsy hand on his mother's shoulder. "He'll be all right, Mama. I will say a prayer for him."

"Yah, prayer is good." Freni turned and grabbed my arm, her tiny fingers drilling into me like steel bits. "I must stay here to be near my Mose, so, Magdalena, it is up to you."

"What is?"

"You must find my missing baby!"

"Me? What about Jonathan?"

"My Jonathan, he must return to his babies."

"And to his wife, Barbara."

Freni flinched. "Yah, to her as well. So you see, Magdalena, only you have the time to look for Little Freni."

"But I don't have time!" I wailed. "I have an inn full of guests and—ouch!" The steel fingers were about to strike bone.

"You'll find her?"

"I'll do my best, but—ah—stop that!"

"Do you promise?"

"I'll find Little Freni!" I shrieked.

Freni smiled. A Yoder, she knew, never breaks a promise.

Well, we almost never break a promise. I promised to love and honor Aaron until death did us part, but I didn't know at that time that he was already married. As a little girl I promised our parents that I would always look out for my baby sister, but how was I to know she would never grow up? And of course I've promised myself a lot of things that have never come to pass. But in general, one can count on a Yoder's word.

Freni, the poor dear, found a folding chair and parked it in front of the examining-room door. Jonathan hoofed it back to the maternity ward, and I hoofed after him. I wish with all my heart Freni had been along. Her beloved son didn't even peek through the nursery window, but headed straight to his wife's side. When I saw how tenderly they greeted each other, I turned and retraced my steps to the nursery.

Little Mose and Little Jonathan were the only two babies in the room. They occupied adjacent incubators, and the baby on the right was being attended to by a nurse with obviously bleached blond hair. She saw me watching her through the window and beckoned to me.

I hesitated at the door. "I can't come in. If Nurse Dudley sees me in there, I'm history."

The blond nurse laughed. "I can fix that." She walked over to a nearby desk, pushed a button, and the drapes closed. "Now put these on." She handed me an ugly green gown and mask.

I did as I was bade and was straightaway led to the incubators. I stared in wonder at the newborns.

"They're so tiny," I said in awe. Believe me, I wasn't going to say they were cute. Only one baby that I know of—*moi*—was ever born cute, and my looks have gone steadily downhill since then.

"Actually, they're very large for twins. This one weighs five pounds eight ounces, and his brother a whopping six pounds two. They actually don't need to be in incubators. It's just a precaution."

"Which one is which?"

"I beg your pardon?" Her eyes, over the mask, seemed strangely familiar.

"I mean, which one is Little Jonathan and which one is Little Mose?"

"That hasn't been decided yet. For now we have them labeled as Baby Hostetler number one, and Baby Hostetler number two."

I stared at the tiny, squished faces. Neither of them looked like their parents, and they both looked more like Freni than Mose. Of course, at that age most babies look like dried apricots.

"Were you the attending nurse at their birth?"

She nodded. "I'm the *only* nurse on duty tonight in

maternity. In case you haven't noticed, this is a very small hospital."

"I've noticed, dear," I said calmly, "but we're fortunate to have it, aren't we?"

"Oh, yes," she said, "don't get me wrong. It's just that where I come from—Pittsburgh—this wouldn't even be considered a clinic. Still, I guess for a one-horse town like this, it beats nothing."

One-horse town indeed! With all the Amish in the area, Hernia is far from being a one-horse town. I refrained from telling the uppity nurse that maybe she ought to go back to Pittsburgh. Instead I made note of her name. *Hemingway.*

"Nurse Hemingway," I said, still calm and collected, "there seems to be some confusion. I accompanied Barbara to her doctor on several occasions, and I'm sure she was supposed to have triplets. There wasn't— I mean, one of the babies wasn't stillborn, was it?"

The familiar eyes, which were far too heavily made-up, glanced at the door before returning to me. "I can assure you, there were just these two very healthy boys."

"Is it possible then that ultrasound pictures could be wrong?"

She shrugged. "Did you see those pictures?"

"Well, not personally. But Barbara did."

Nurse Hemingway glanced at the door again. "Doctors sometime make mistakes."

"You don't say!" I was, of course, being facetious. I have great respect for doctors, but have never believed them to be infallible—well, not since the day one left a surgical glove and six feet of gauze inside my Uncle Ernie in an attempt to remove a tumor he didn't have.

Nurse Hemingway nodded. "You wouldn't believe some of the things I've seen. Who was Mrs. Hostetler's original OB-GYN?"

"Dr. Pierce up in Bedford. Do you know him?"

"Let's just say I've heard a few things about the man."

"Like what?"

"Well, far be it for me to spread tales out of school"—she chuckled—"I mean, the hospital, *but*—"

"Spit it out, dear!"

"Well, I've only been in the area a short time, but it didn't take long for me to hear about his liquid lunches."

"Slim-Fast?"

"Martinis don't make you slim. Fast or slow."

"He was a drinker?"

"World class, from what I hear."

"Oh. Well, I suppose that could impair his judgment. Poor Barbara."

"Yes, I imagine she is disappointed. But two healthy baby boys, that's something for which anyone should be grateful."

"You don't think her health was impaired—or the babies—by Dr. Pierce's prenatal care early on?"

"I don't see how. Besides, as I understand it, she's been seeing Dr. Bauer for the last couple of months."

"Could you tell me where to find Dr. Bauer?"

Nurse Hemingway blinked. "What's the matter? Don't you think I know what I'm talking about? I may be a blonde, but I can count to three, you know."

I was taken aback by the abrupt change in her demeanor. I was also feeling a good deal of stress.

"I'm sure you can count to three. No doubt you can

even arrange M&M's in alphabetical order. But I still want to speak with Dr. Bauer."

She stared at me through unnaturally thick lashes. "You can probably find Dr. Bauer down the hall to your left. His name is on his office. Oh, you can read, can't you, Mrs. Hostetler?"

"Mrs. *Hostetler*?"

"Aren't you Jonathan's mother? I mean, these are your grandbabies, aren't they?"

"Why I never! Jonathan's only twelve years younger than I!"

"Ah, then you're Barbara's mother."

"Why I never!" I said and stamped from the room, still wearing the gown and mask.

I knocked softly on Dr. Bauer's door, which was closed. When he didn't answer, I knocked appropriately louder. A strip of light shone under the door, and I could hear grunting. I knocked again, this time loud enough to wake the dead (Trust me, the Good Lord could use someone like me at resurrection time). The answering grunt was commensurately loud, and I chose to interpret it as an invitation to enter.

My opening the door seemed to catch Dr. Bauer by surprise. Heaven knows I was surprised. There, behind a massive wooden desk, sat a white-haired gnome. An ancient, wizened white-haired gnome. I mean, it is one thing to have an experienced doctor, but *this* man had no doubt known God as a boy.

I stared stupidly, my mouth open wide enough to catch a barn swallow. As I stared I happened to notice the gnome had a needle in his arm. He appeared to be giving himself some sort of injection.

"Yes?" he snapped.

I closed my mouth, and gave my lips a few trial flaps before attempting speech. "Are you Dr. Bauer?"

He nodded at the needle. "I'm a diabetic. In my case it can't be controlled by oral medication."

"Oh. Sorry to hear that. Dr. Bauer, do you mind if I ask you a few questions?"

"Are you a doctor?"

"No."

"Nurse?"

"No."

"Then why are you dressed like that?"

I pulled the mask down to expose my face. "I was in to see the Hostetler babies."

He nodded. "Come in, Mrs. Hostetler."

"I am *not* Mrs. Hostetler," I wailed. "I'm Magdalena Yoder."

Behind thick lenses, tiny eyes lit up like illuminated beads. "Not *the* Magdalena Yoder of the PennDutch Inn?"

"One and the same!" I cried, delighted that someone—anyone—would recognize my name. "Do I know you?"

"No, I'm afraid not. But my wife and I have been trying for years to get a reservation at your inn."

I flushed. Until just recently my inn was the haunt of the rich and famous and I could afford to be as picky as a baboon with fleas. I mean, *everyone* who was *anyone* stayed there. Babs, Brad, Bill—you name it, although the latter was in my face just a bit too much. Anyway, not much more than a year ago my precious PennDutch was flattened by a tornado and I was forced to rebuild. The new version is identical to the old, but somehow it seems to have lost its charisma. Folks are no longer "charmed" by it. My guests these days are sociology professors and factory workers from England.

I smiled at the dinky doc. "Try again, dear. I'm sure
I'll be able to fit you and your wife in—at the inn." I
laughed pleasantly. "That was a little joke. Did you
get it?"

"Marla passed away two years ago."

"Oh. Uh, well, if you still want to stay with me, you
just name the date. In fact, I'll let you stay for free."

Dr. Bauer twirled one end of a snow-white mustache. "Why would I want to do that? I live here
now."

"Then I guess you wouldn't, not unless you wanted
a week of maid service and the best home cooking
this side of the Mississippi."

"Three meals a day?"

"Yes, but they're at set hours. None of this eating
on the run that's so fashionable these days."

The elfin physician smiled. "Sounds good to me.
When?"

"Like I said, you name it. But first I'd like to ask
you a few questions."

He folded hands that were even smaller than
Freni's. "Ask away."

"It's about the Hostetler babies. You delivered
them, right?"

"That's correct."

"And there were two to begin with?"

He smiled, revealing the tiniest teeth I had ever
seen on an adult human being. They were smaller
even than baby teeth. Weasel teeth is what they were.

"Of course there were two. I'm not in the habit of
throwing in an extra baby for good measure."

"No, that's not what I meant. You see, I'm positive—well, pretty sure—that Barbara Hostetler was supposed to be carrying triplets."

Dr. Bauer laughed. He sounded more like Santa than a weasel.

"Triplets? That's preposterous. Those babies were almost full term, with normal birth weights. A woman would have to be as big and strong as a horse to carry triplets that long."

"Which Barbara is," I said, not unkindly. A fact is a fact, after all. Barbara Kauffman Hostetler stands six feet tall in her woolen stockings. Her limbs are as thick and sturdy as my porch columns, and she has never been sick a day in her life. True, she was as barren as the Gobi Desert for the first twenty years of her marriage, but I personally think that is only because it took that long for the seed to reach fertile ground—if you know what I mean.

"Nevertheless, she delivered twins. I'm filling in the forms right now. Would you like to see them?"

I sighed. "That's not necessary. Well, I guess Dr. Pierce was mistaken."

Beady eyes burned brighter. "What do you mean?"

"Well, according to Barbara, Dr. Pierce said he heard three little hearts beating inside her."

"There were just two."

"You're positive?" I half expected him to go ballistic at the question, but he remained surprisingly calm.

"Barbara Hostetler has been under my care since the beginning of her second trimester. I am quite sure."

I sighed again. "Well, either Dr. Pierce was just plain incompetent, or he was the heavy drinker I hear he was."

"No comment."

A jolt of adrenaline made me stand ramrod-straight. "Which is exactly what you just did. Dr. Ignacious Pierce *is* an incompetent, isn't he?"

"I didn't say that."

"Then he's a heavy drinker!"

This time Santa smiled without showing me his teeth.

"Thank you," I said. "You've been a big help."

"My pleasure. I'll be calling you about my free stay at the PennDutch."

"You do that."

I left feeling ambivalent about my encounter with the white-haired gnome. I could think of no reason why the man should lie to me, but my gut was telling me that something was wrong. But either Dr. Bauer was telling the truth, or he was as smooth as Freni's butterscotch chiffon pie. Pie! Good heavens! It was lunchtime already, and I had an inn full of guests, but no cook. I ran to find Freni, and straight into a new set of problems.

Five

Freni's Butterscotch Chiffon Pie

✦

½ cup cold water
1 envelope unflavored gelatin
4 teaspoons instant coffee powder
¼ teaspoon salt
2 eggs, separated
1 package (6 ounces) butterscotch pieces
½ cup firmly packed light brown sugar
1 cup whipping cream

1 baked nine-inch pie shell

Combine water, gelatin, coffee, and salt in saucepan. Cook and stir over moderate heat until gelatin dissolves and mixture comes to a boil. Remove from heat. Beat egg yolks slightly; add gelatin mixture gradually, stirring rapidly. Cook over low heat one minute, stirring constantly. Remove from heat. Stir in butterscotch pieces, reserving one tablespoon for garnish. Beat egg whites until stiff; beat in brown sugar. Continue to beat until stiff and satiny. Fold in butterscotch mixture. Whip cream; reserve half cup for garnish. Fold in remainder. Spoon into pie shell. Garnish. Chill until set.

Serves eight English or four Mennonites or two Amish.

Six

"**F**reni went *where*?" I wailed.

Nurse Dudley glared at me. "Dr. Luther already told you. She went to Bedford Community Hospital to be with her husband. That nice Mennonite man drove her."

"*Why?*"

"Because our policy is not to allow family members to ride along with critical cases. It's too distracting to the medics."

"I know that, you, you—" I prayed and swallowed the word *twit*. "What I want to know is, why did Mose have to go to Bedford for his surgery? Why couldn't he have it here?"

Dr. Luther smiled. He seemed every bit as sincere as a Cheshire cat.

"The patient—Mose Hostetler—is suffering from acute appendicitis. It may already be ruptured. And like I said before—"

"Indeed you did," Nurse Dudley said.

It was my turn to glare at her. "Please, let the doctor continue."

Dr. Luther nodded in agreement, sending Nurse Dudley into a snit. Fortunately for all concerned she retreated behind the admissions desk to lick her wounds.

"Miss Yoder, like I said before, we are a very small hospital. We have only one anesthesiologist and she's on vacation."

"But so are my guests, and they're expecting lunch! At least if Mose was here, I could shuttle Freni back and forth in a matter of minutes."

"Perhaps you could cook for them," he said, and didn't even crack a smile.

"Fried ice and doughnut holes are my specialties," I said bitterly. Mama ruled her kitchen with a cast-iron fist. I was never allowed to help because I was *dabbrich und strubbly*—clumsy and messy. As a consequence, I've been known to burn water.

"Fried ice and doughnut holes are a vast improvement over my wife's cooking," Dr. Luther said with the barest hint of a smile. "Last night she served curried goat."

"Is she looking for a job?"

He laughed. "That's a good one."

"No, I'm serious." I'd tell this bunch that goat was an Amish delicacy, and no one would be the wiser except for the helpful Redigers, and since Mennonites will eat anything, goat was not going to be a problem.

"You're such a kidder, Ms. Yoder. But all joking aside, there is something you might be able to do to make sure a situation like this doesn't arise again."

"How many appendixes does Mose have?"

"Huh? Oh, you're joking again!"

"I most certainly am not! Now, if you'll excuse me—" I didn't have time for this. I tried to make a run for the door, but Dr. Luther was a surprisingly nimble man. He was bobbing and weaving in front of me like a pugilist.

"Look," he said, panting, "it's this. If we had a world-renown heart surgeon on staff, we could attract other qualified personnel."

"Oh, I get it! You want me to get my boyfriend on board. Well, do I at least get a finder's fee?"

"Hmm. I hadn't thought of that. Perhaps something could be arranged, but more along the lines of a discount."

"That could work." After all, as a privately employed person, my health benefits are not all that great. "How much of a discount, and on what?"

"Well, I've been negotiating with a plastic surgeon in Scranton—"

"A plastic surgeon?"

"Well, I just assumed you wanted to do something about that nose."

"Look, Nurse Dudley's naked!" I cried, and in the second it took for him to look, I was out the door.

Plastic surgeon indeed! I have never—okay, but with diminishing frequency—been so insulted. I may not have the perfect proboscis, but I'll have you know that during her last stay at the PennDutch, Babs told me she wanted one just like it. No, sir, I may not be Helen of Troy, but I am not a homely woman. To the contrary, I am a comely woman, known to have lit fires in the loins of at least one man.

And what's more, I have a modicum of brains. I jumped into my sinfully red BMW and raced for Sam Yoder's Corner Market.

*   *   *

Thank heavens the Good Lord in His mercy had seen fit to create frozen dinners. But did He have to make so many?

"Which kind is the best?" I wailed.

My cousin, Sam Yoder, shook his head. "I can't believe my ears. You're going to serve this crap at the PennDutch Inn?"

"Please, watch your language, dear. And if they're so awful, then why do you sell them?"

"Money," Sam said, digging around in an immense freezer at the back of his store. He straightened. "Here. These are the best. Add enough cheese of your own and the lasagna is passable. And try the beef tips with mashed potatoes. Stir a little real cream and butter into those spuds, and they're not too bad. And this frozen corn tastes pretty much like the real thing if you don't know any better. Just remember to put everything into serving bowls."

"Of course, dear, I'm not a total idiot."

Sam rolled his eyes behind frosty lashes. "Uh-huh."

"All right! So once—just once—I tried to heat beans without opening the can."

Sam chuckled. "At least you got a new skylight out of that experience. When my Dorothy first tried canning with a pressure cooker, she took off the roof."

"Your wife is a Methodist, dear. She's not supposed to know how to cook."

"Very funny. So what gives, Magdalena? Freni quit on you for the one-millionth time?"

"It's only been ninety-six times, dear, and no, she didn't quit. Mose is having his appendix removed over in Bedford."

"Ouch. Is it serious?"

"Could be. But can you believe the timing? And

Barbara can't come over and help because she just had twins."

Sam's eyes widened. "Already? And you mean triplets, don't you?"

"*Twins.* Only Freni's having a hard time accepting that. Apparently Barbara's doctor made a mistake."

"What's his name?"

"Pierce. Dr. Ignacious Pierce."

"Old Red?'

"*Pierce,* dear," I hissed. The frozen dinners were hurting my hands and making me crabby.

"Yes, I know his real name, but I play poker with him Tuesdays and we call him Old Red because he can polish off a bottle of Johnnie Walker Red in one night—by *himself.* Besides, he has red hair."

I gasped. "Why shame on you, Samuel Elias Yoder! Playing cards and drinking!"

"I'm a Methodist now, remember? I'm allowed to drink, just as long as I feel guilty about it."

I waggled a finger at him. "Just the same, your parents would be turning over in their graves if they could see you now."

"Well, they can't. And even if they can, I'm sure they have better things to occupy themselves with than my one night of pleasure each week. It's Old Red's patients who have something to worry about. I've known in my gut for a long time something bad was going to happen, and now it has. Losing a baby in the delivery room is a whole lot more serious than forgetting to order extra bread for the holidays."

"Old Red—I mean, Dr. Pierce—didn't deliver Barbara's babies. It was a very short labor. She practically spit those boys out on the way to Hernia Hospital. A Dr. Bauer finished the job."

"Boys, did you say?"

"Little Mose and Little Jonathan."

"Is Freni fit to be tied?" he asked. Neither Sam nor I could resist snide smiles.

"Well, she would be, if she wasn't convinced that Little Freni is out there somewhere."

"Where?"

"That's what I'm supposed to find out. I know everything's been happening ahead of schedule, but it's too much to ask me to believe that Little Freni just hopped off the delivery table and ran out of the room."

"Maybe her guardian angels clued her in about Big Freni."

We both laughed. It was wicked of us, and I'm truly sorry now. But we were younger then, were we not? Besides, Freni brings a lot of her troubles on herself, what with her sharp tongue and rigid ways.

I tried sneaking into my own kitchen, my arms laden with state-of-the-art TV dinners. One should not have to be furtive in one's own home, but guests routinely ignore the NO TRESPASSING sign on the kitchen door. This batch of guests was no different.

"What are you doing in here?" I demanded of Professor Barnes. He was still wearing the shabby suit and cheap tie, but a lot of his uniform was now covered by Freni's best white apron.

"I'm making lunch."

I shuffled my packages behind me, dropped them on the floor, and spread my skirt like a screen. "But you can't!"

"Why not? Because I haven't paid extra for the privilege of cooking?"

The Moregold twins, also clad in Freni's aprons, giggled. My impulse was to glare at them, but I wasn't about to ruin my chances to sample a genuine English cream tea later in the day.

"We were hungry," Daphne said. "I guess our bodies haven't fully adjusted to American time."

Professor Barnes pushed the frayed cuff of his suit. "It's two thirty-three. Even in America this is late for lunch."

I glanced at the counter. Everything in Freni's fridge was piled there.

"What are you making?"

"Scrambled eggs with cheese," the professor said. "As for the bizarre concoction these ladies are making, you'll have to ask them."

"It's bubble and squeak," Daphne chirped.

"Come again?"

"Fried greens and leftover potatoes," Edwina explained. "We call it that in England because of the sound it makes when it cooks."

"It goes very well with toad-in-the-hole," Daphne said, "but we couldn't find any sausages."

"I see. Well, I guess I had the last for breakfast. Say, where are the others?"

The twins giggled.

"What's so funny, dears?"

"You mean the honeymooners?" Daphne asked.

I shuddered, remembering Vivian Mays and her boy-toy Sandy. "How did you know they were honeymooners?"

"All that racket. Edwina and I were afraid at first it might be an earthquake. It would be our very first, you know?"

"If they break my bed they're going to pay for it," I wailed.

"I shouldn't think they'd be coming out of their room anytime soon," Edwina said, and stirred the mess in her skillet. It did indeed bubble and squeak.

"Give them three minutes," I said, speaking from experience.

"Times ten," Daphne said. "I've never heard such energy."

Professor Barnes wiped albumen on Freni's apron. "And then there's your mystery guest."

"Mystery guest?"

"He checked in about twenty minutes ago. I made him sign the register, but he merely scribbled."

"You *what*?"

"Oh, should I have paid for the privilege of doing that?"

Daphne and Edwina squealed with laughter. I put the cream tea in jeopardy and glared at them. I had forgotten about my last guest. He had called the week before to make reservations, but the man mumbled like he had a mouth full of marbles—at least I think it was a man. At any rate, it was all I could do to decipher a first name. Pelvis! Now, what kind of a name is that? When I got off the phone I had no idea where Pelvis was from, or even which credit card he planned to use.

"What does Pelvis look like?"

Professor Barnes reached for a whisk. "He was dressed in black. Black pants, black shirt, black hat. He was even wearing black gloves."

Gloves? In the summer? That could only mean one person.

"Was he wearing one glove or two?"

Watering gray eyes scrutinized me under hedgerow brows. "Two, of course. Otherwise I would have said *glove.*"

Well, two gloves weren't going to fool me. Pelvis indeed! No doubt Moonwalker was too much of a giveaway.

"What did Pelvis's face look like?" I managed to ask casually.

"I don't know. He was wearing a black ski mask. You have some strange guests, Miss Yoder."

"Tell me about it."

"I think Pelvis is in mourning," Edwina said. "Daph and I heard weeping."

Daphne giggled inappropriately. "Actually, sis, I think that sound was coming from the honeymoon suite."

I waved at her to be quiet. "Professor Barnes, surely you can tell me more than that. For instance, was he tall? Short? Fat? Thin?"

"Well, it wasn't Elvis, if that's what you're thinking."

The Moregolds twittered.

Encouraged, the professor pushed his luck. "Contrary to what you may read in the tabloids, Miss Yoder, Elvis Presley is dead."

I smiled pleasantly. "No, of course it wasn't Elvis Presley. *He* lives in a cottage behind the barn."

Daphne and Edwina exchanged glances.

"Does he really?" Daphne asked.

"Oh, yes. But he shares the cottage with Jimmy Hoffa."

They looked at me uncomprehendingly.

"Never mind. Is there enough food there for my three other guests as well?"

"Plenty of bubble and squeak," Edwina said.

"Same with the eggs," the professor said grudgingly.

"Good. Be a dear, will you, and make up three plates to take upstairs."

Then, ignoring the inevitable complaints, I scooped up my packages from Sam and fled to the basement freezer. It was time for me to check out the mystery guest.

Seven

I left a tray for the honeymooners first.

"Lunch is outside your door," I called. "I'll be back to pick up your tray in half an hour. Eat now, or forget it."

There was no response. I moved down the hall and set the tray in front of the mystery guest's room. Then I knocked softly.

"Jacko, is that you?" I whispered. The man is a favorite of mine, ever since he let me pet his llama.

Silence.

"I promise not to tell a soul." Of course I would— but long after the guest had departed. So you see, it really wouldn't be the same as lying. At any rate, once word got out that an entertainer of his stature had stayed at the *new* PennDutch Inn, celebrities would return like swallows to Capistrano.

There was no response.

"I know the media has treated you horridly, dear. But I'm your friend, remember? I helped you pick out baby names."

Either my guest was asleep or in the bathroom.

I knocked again, this time louder. Much to my surprise, the door swung open. Much to my dismay, the room was empty.

"This can't be!" I lurched into the room, and in the process tripped over the lunch tray, scattering scrambled eggs and bubble and squeak all over a freshly waxed hardwood floor. Ignoring the mess, I ran to the bathroom. It too was empty.

"Darn!" I said, which is as bad as I can swear.

"Is there a problem?"

I whirled. Sandy Roberts was standing in the hallway, one of my admittedly threadbare towels his only garment. His supple young body gleamed in the overhead light.

I looked away. "This doesn't concern you, dear."

"Yeah, well, if there is a problem, you let me know. I didn't like the looks of that guy."

"So it *is* a guy?"

"Yeah, I guess so. It was kind of hard to tell. It was all those black clothes I didn't like. Too depressing."

"At least he's wearing clothes, dear."

"Hey, I only came out here because I thought you might need some help."

One of Mama's favorite sayings was the one about using honey, instead of vinegar, to catch flies. Mama, incidentally, rarely caught flies. Not that *I* wanted to catch flies, mind you. It's just that it never hurts to have a spy working for you.

"Your help is very much appreciated, dear. In fact, I'd be grateful if you alerted me the next time you saw him."

I sneaked a peek just long enough to see him nod. "Yeah, okay."

"Thanks, dear." I bent over to pick up the tray and what remained of Jacko's lunch.

"Here let me help you."

I will not burden you with the details of what happened next. Suffice it to say, when young Sandy squatted to help, my threadbare towel gave away and I saw more of the man than I've seen of any man, with the possible exception of my erstwhile, ersatz husband.

"Aack!" I squawked.

The door behind Sandy swung open. Vivian Mays stood there, dressed in little more than her gold chains.

"What's going on—what the hell?" She made no move to cover her nakedness.

"It's not what it looks like," I wailed. "I mean, I'm sure it's real, but that's not what I mean!"

"What *do* you mean?" Vivian Mays sounded like Mama, Reverend Shrock, and my third-grade schoolteacher rolled into one.

"I mean I was only asking your husband to help me spy on Michael Jackson—" I clapped a hand over my mouth, snatched up the empty tray, and fled down my impossibly steep stairs. Just as I reached the bottom, the phone rang.

I picked up in my bedroom. It was my private line.

"Hello?"

Silence.

"Jacko, is that you?"

"Jackal?" I heard a faint voice say. "Magdalena, are you off your rocket again?"

"Freni! Turn the receiver around, and that's rocker, not rocket."

While Freni fumbled with the phone, I prayed for patience. The woman is metaphorically, as well as mechanically, challenged. The latter is not her fault, however. As an Amish woman she does not own a telephone, nor does she own any electrically operated appliances.

"Magdalena?" she said, her voice normal at last. "Are you there?"

"Yes, dear. What's up? How's Mose?"

"Ach, my Mose. The doctor said his appendix was ready to burst. Red hot, he said, like a tamale. What is this tamale?"

"I think it's a food, dear. So it hadn't yet burst?"

"No, thank God. They're operating now."

"Are you scared?"

She didn't hesitate. "Yah."

"Hang on, dear, I'll be there as soon as I can. I'm leaving right now."

"Ach, but what about the English? Who will feed them?"

"They're feeding themselves."

"Ach!" Freni must have dropped the phone, because I could have done *The New York Times* crossword puzzle in the time it took her to speak again. "My kitchen," she gasped. "There are English in my kitchen?"

"Well, maybe not at this very moment, but there were. And frankly, dear, they seemed to be having fun."

"Cooking on my stove with my pots and pans?"

"Technically, dear, they're my pots and pans."

She paused again, but her heavy breathing made it clear she was still on the line. "What did they cook?"

"Bubble and squeak."

"Ach, jokes, Magdalena, when my Mose is dying."
"Dying?"

"Maybe not dying, but he's an old man. The doctor—speak of the doctor, there's the devil now."

"What?"

The phone banged against something as she literally left me hanging. I thought of disconnecting and trying again, but unless she replaced the receiver, there was no point. Besides, there was no way to tell which number she was calling from. I did the only thing I could and remained on the line. After the same amount of time it would take me to translate *The New York Times* crossword puzzle into Japanese, Freni got back on the line.

"Magdalena," she said, as if she'd never left me dangling, "it's good news. The doctor said the operation is over and my Mose did well. The hot tamale is gone."

"Thank God!"

"Yah. Now he must recover for an hour."

"Just an hour?"

"Yah, and then they put him in a private room, or a public room. Which room do we want, Magdalena?"

"Nothing's too good for our Mose. Get the private. But don't worry about a thing, Freni. I'll be right there."

"Ach, there's no need for that. Donald will help me."

"Donald?"

"That nice Mennonite man."

"Donald Rediger is still with you? Where's his wife?"

"Yah, Donald is here. His wife went shopping— things for my babies. Ach, such nice people. You should have more guests like them, Magdalena."

I bit my tongue. Freni's favorite guest over the years has been a movie star with a Mennonite name. But while Mel might be a good Mennonite name, that's one brave heart who is not of the faith.

"I'm grateful to the Redigers," I said calmly, "but they're not family. I'll be there in a jiffy."

"No!"

"What do you mean 'no'?"

"The doctor said my Mose is going to be okay. You have other things to do."

"Of course, dear, but none of them is as important as looking after you and Mose." You see? A human heart does beat beneath this bony breast! That article in the *National Intruder* was wrong.

"Yah, Magdalena, there is someone more important than me. Even than my Mose—"

"Freni, dear, Jonathan and the twins are fine."

"Yah, thank God. I mean someone else."

"Barbara?" How refreshing. Freni had been a grandmother for only a few short hours, but already she'd softened.

"Ach, not Barbara! Little Freni."

I sighed. "Freni, there's no good way to tell you this, except to come right out and say it—there never was a Little Freni."

While Freni fumbled again, I kept my ear a safe six inches from the receiver. Finally she got back on. Her first sentence was in Pennsylvania Dutch, so I can't repeat it. Her second sentence was in English, but it doesn't bear repeating.

"Calm down, dear," I said gently. "Just give it some time to sink in. You'll get used to the idea."

"I will not!"

"You have two healthy grandsons, Freni. You should count your blessings."

"Yah, I count them. One, two, *three*!"

"Freni, before I left Hernia Hospital I spoke to both the delivery-room doctor and the nurse. They confirmed it. There never was a Little Freni."

"There *is*! Make them take a polygamy test."

"A *what*?"

"A test to tell the truth."

"Ah, a polygraph! Freni, dear, that simply isn't how things work."

"Do you believe them, Magdalena?"

I took a deep breath. "I see no reason not to."

"Ach, but maybe the doctor made a mistake."

"Freni, the doctor knows how many babies he delivered."

"The doctor is a *dummkopf*."

By rights I should have dropped the phone. A good Amish woman, Freni never swears. Her sharp tongue gets honed through criticism and insinuation. I'm sure there are those who would not consider dumbhead a swear word, but in Freni's world it ranks right up there with "darn."

"Tch, tch," I clucked self-righteously. "You've never even met the man."

"Yah, but what he says is stupid. I know my Little Freni exists. I can feel it in my stomach."

"You mean in your gut?" Heaven forfend Freni should come down with a sympathetic pregnancy.

"Yah, in my gut. So, Magdalena, will you find my little granddaughter?"

"I'll do my best," I promised wearily.

"Yah, your best. Your mama would be proud of you, Magdalena."

"Really?"

"Yah. You aren't selfish after all."

"Mama said I was?"

"Ach! They're ready to move Mose to his room," she said and hung up.

"But it hasn't been an hour," I wailed to the dial tone. "It's hardly been five minutes."

Then in a quirk that only Pennsylvania Bell can explain, the dial tone hung up on me as well. I am ashamed to admit what happened next. I didn't exactly throw the phone, but I did drop it from a considerable height and with more force than I'd intended. The fact that the casing cracked and the machine was rendered permanently inoperable was my fault, not Ma Bell's.

I had no choice but to leave the safety of my room and use the front desk phone. I had barely gone the length of my nose when I was ambushed.

"Miss Yoder!"

I jumped a good two inches. This happens a lot to me, but I have learned over the years that as long as I restrict the lateral movements, no one notices. Drawing on my experience, I was able to appear practically nonchalant. The interloper, incidentally, was Vivian Mays. She was at least covered now, but her filmy wrap showed more details of her topography than I cared to know.

"Yes?" I said, even managing a slight smile.

"Did you think you could get away with it?" she demanded.

"I paid for it," I said calmly. "I'll do what I want with it."

"And you call yourself Amish!"

"Actually, I don't. My ancestors were Amish—up until my grandparents' generation—but I belong to Beechy Grove Mennonite Church. We're allowed to own telephones. Even computers."

"Is that how you met? On the Internet?"

"Met who, dear?"

"My husband!"

"Your *husband*?"

"Don't play games with me. I caught you red-handed, remember? So how much did you pay him?"

I suddenly realized what she meant and flushed. "I didn't pay for him! I paid for my phone."

She stared at me. "Either you're clueless, or a world-class liar."

"I couldn't lie my way through a mattress makers' convention," I wailed.

"You want me to believe you didn't arrange a rendezvous with my Sandy?"

"I wouldn't touch your boy-toy with a ten-foot pole. I have my own fellow—an adult."

"Then what were you doing across from our room?"

"Checking on a guest, not that it's any of your business. More to the point, what were you doing opening your door clad only in your birthday suit?"

"Sandy and I are nudists, not that it's any of your business."

"*What?* You better explain, toots, or you're out on your ear."

That seemed to shake her. No doubt Vivian's ears had already been given a workout.

"We met at a nude rally last month," she said. "*Nudes for Nukes*. It's a pro-nuclear energy movement. If we don't stop burning nonrenewable resources, like fossil fuels, this planet is in big trouble. But don't worry, Miss Yoder, we don't plan to walk around your inn in our natural states. We—I—kind of forgot myself there."

I took several deep breaths and counted to ten in Spanish before responding. Words, unlike cheap, thoughtless Christmas presents, cannot be taken back.

"See that you don't parade around in the buff," I puffed. "I am a good Christian woman and decent folks stay here." Well, half of that statement was true.

Vivian Mays nodded. "It won't happen again. So, can we just put that little scene behind us?"

I didn't like the woman. They say we automatically dislike twenty percent of the people we meet based solely on physical characteristics. These are often minutiae of which we may not even be aware. So why is it that I seem to dislike a far higher percentage of my guests? First the pompous Dr. Barnes, and now a rude nude! Still, on one level, I had to admire a woman that old who not only let it all hang out, but in doing so, caught a man half her age.

"Consider it forgotten," I said. But I spoke too soon.

Eight

I looked up Dr. Ignacious Pierce's office in the Bedford directory. I called and got the machine. In the background there was Christmas music, for crying out loud. In July!

"We are out of the office for the duration of the holidays. If this is an emergency, you may call 555-2139."

Dr. Pierce didn't seem to be home either. The machine issued a cryptic command, and before I could open my mouth, I was disconnected. A more superstitious person might well have concluded that Alexander Graham Bell had it in for me.

Fortunately I remembered Barbara mentioning the name of Dr. Pierce's nurse—Melba Mast. The Mast family forms a long limb on my family tree, and Melba is one of the twigs of my generation. Actually, she is several twigs. The woman is my fourth cousin nine different ways, which by my reckoning makes her the equivalent of a first cousin with one part left over. Quite possibly she is a sister I never realized I had. At any rate, I knew that like me, the woman had never legally married, so finding her name in the phone book was no problem. However, as you may well understand, I elected to drive over rather than dial.

Melba Mast lives on Maple Street, in the heart of historic Hernia. Hers is a white, gingerbread Victorian house, replete with turret and fish-scale shingles. Atop the turret is a weather vane, although instead of a cock, this one sports a cat. The sidewalk that leads to her house is bordered by beds of alternating red, white, and blue flowers. An ancient maple shades the left side of her lawn, a Colorado blue spruce dominates the right. A pair of wooden Dutch children steal a kiss on the maple side, and on the spruce side a two-dimensional woman displays her bloomers.

It took Melba several minutes to answer the door, and when she did, I was hit in the face by a wave of rancid air.

"Yes?"

I struggled to remain standing. "Miss Mast, I'm Magdalena Yoder, third cousin once removed from Freni Hostetler who is Barbara Hostetler's mother-in-law."

"Come in," Melba said. She almost seemed eager to have company.

I looked longingly at two white wicker rockers that graced the porch. It was a perfect summer day, around eighty degrees, with low humidity. However, it would have been rude to direct the hostess, and besides, I did want to see what was inside.

Cats. That's what was inside. Dozens of cats in all colors and sizes. They were asleep on the antique furniture, grooming themselves, nibbling out of bowls, and in one instance, using a philodendron pot as a litter box. Frankly, judging by the odor of the place,

I wouldn't have been surprised to learn that one or two of the kitties was caput.

"How many cats do you have, dear?" I asked, without sounding judgmental.

"Thirty-two, if you count Caspar. But he really belongs to my boss who is on vacation. Most of the others were strays that I've taken in over the years. The kittens you see have all been abandoned. All my pussies are either spayed or neutered."

I was born and raised on a farm and like animals of all descriptions—except for the two-pound pooch my sister Susannah carries around in her bra. That miserable mite is eighty percent jaws and twenty percent sphincter muscle. At any rate, I even like cats. Just not thirty-two of them in the same place.

"You must be a remarkable woman," I said charitably.

"Thanks. Have a seat." She picked up an enormous black Persian and set him gently on the floor.

I sat gingerly. There was so much matted cat hair on the Victorian sofa that the seat was slippery. Beside me was a short-haired calico, above me on the narrow edge of the back seat was a wedge-faced Siamese, and perched on the padded armrest was a brown striped tabby.

Melba evicted an orange cat from a side chair opposite me and sat, placing the cat in her lap. "It is so nice to have visitors, isn't it, Ginger?" she cooed.

Ginger meowed, and Melba meowed back.

"Do they all have names?" I asked foolishly.

"Oh, yes. That's Patches on the seat beside you, Tiddlywinks on the armrest, and Ming behind you."

"It's amazing how Ming can cling to such a narrow perch."

"He loves high places. Did you know that Siamese cats were originally bred to ride into battle on the shoulders of Siamese warriors? The cats were trained to leap into the enemy's face and scratch their eyes."

I leaned forward. "How charming."

"Oh, Ming would never hurt you. You're a real puddy-tat, aren't you, Ming? Yes, you are, yes you are."

I wanted to puke, but of course I didn't. Had I, the stench would not have been noticeable.

"Melba, dear, like I said before, I'm a distant cousin by marriage to Barbara Hostetler. What I didn't mention was that I consider her a close friend, and her mother-in-law—well, Freni is like a second mother to me. Anyway, we were all pretty sure that Barbara was going to have triplets. In fact, we were positive that was the case."

Melba was an attractive woman my age, which just goes to show you that not all of us are single by default. "Yes, Barbara Hostetler is going to have triplets. In fact, they're due any day now."

"They're here—only they're twins, not triplets."

What began as a smile ended as a frown. "I don't understand."

"Barbara delivered this morning, here at Hernia Hospital. But she gave birth to only two babies."

"Are you *sure*?"

"I spoke with her husband Jon who was at the delivery, and with the doctor and nurse as well."

Melba pushed Ginger off her lap and stood. "But that's impossible."

"Is it?"

"Well, at least highly improbable. Doctors do make mistakes, but usually if they make mistakes it's because they miss a baby. Not the other way around. And Dr. Pierce is very good."

"He, uh—well—did he have a fondness for the bottle?"

Surprise, disbelief, outrage, they all took their turns on Melba's comely face. "He most certainly did not!"

"Sorry, dear, but I needed to ask. I've heard that some doctors drink too much."

"Well, not Dr. Pierce. In the twenty years I've worked for him, I never saw him take a drink. Not even when his wife died of cancer three years ago."

"I'm glad to hear that. Not about his wife," I added quickly, "but about the sober part. Melba, did you see Barbara's chart? Did you see the ultrasound pictures?"

Melba shook her head. She had short brown hair streaked with gray and large green eyes. All she needed were a few whiskers for camouflage.

"I saw her chart, but there was never any ultrasound done. Unless there is a problem, many of the Amish around here shun such procedures. Dr. Pierce found those heartbeats the old-fashioned way, with a stethoscope. But like I said he's very good—and sober! If you ask me, it was a shame when Barbara transferred to Dr. Bauer here at Hernia Hospital. Still, I can understand her point of view. Twelve miles into Bedford might not seem like a lot to us, but it can be in a horse and buggy."

The woman had no more experience with a horse and buggy than had I, but I nodded agreeably. She seemed encouraged enough to do a little venting.

"Dr. Pierce lost a lot of patients to that little man."

"Now, now, dear, let's be kind," I said foolishly. "How many patients was it?"

"I'm not at liberty to say."

"Ten, a dozen?"

She glanced around the room, as if challenging her cats to keep a secret. "Two other patients from Hernia alone."

"Yes, but like you said, it's much easier for Amish when there is a doctor based locally."

"Yes, but one of those women wasn't even Amish."

"You don't say? Tell me, where is Dr. Pierce now? The office machine said something about you being closed for the holidays. You do know that Christmas is still a good five and a half months away."

She blushed. "I'm technologically challenged, you see. Dr. Pierce told me to change the message, but I was having trouble with it. So, I found an old tape—well, it still gets the point across, doesn't it?"

"That depends. I was directed to call the doctor at home, but he wasn't there. Is he on vacation?"

Melba was still standing. "Say, do you want any tea? Some milk, maybe?"

"No thanks. But why do I get the feeling you're dodging my question?"

She sat, and immediately the orange cat found his place. "Because I don't know where he is."

"What do you mean?"

"I stayed after work last Friday to use the computer. I don't have one of my own you see, and Iggy—I mean, Dr. Pierce doesn't mind if I use the one at work."

"Do you ski the net?"

"That's *surf*, and yes I do. The last time I checked—which was Friday—there were over a million and a half references to cats, and that was just on Alta Vista.

No doubt other search engines could have turned up more."

"That's fascinating, dear, but can we get back to the subject?"

"Ah, yes. Well, when I signed off the net there was a phone message from Dr. Pierce. In it he said that he had decided to take a long vacation and asked me to change the phone message. But he didn't tell me where he was going. Oh, and of course he told me to take a vacation as well."

"Of course. But isn't that unusual? I mean, for an OB-GYN to just take off like that?"

"It is, but of course doctors always have someone to cover for them."

"Of course. Who did Dr. Pierce have?"

"Well, I really shouldn't be telling you all this . . ."

"I love cats," I purred.

She brightened. "Oh, well, you look like a woman who can be trusted, and it isn't a secret or anything. Dr. Clayton, who has an office next door, sees Dr. Pierce's patients when he has to be away."

"Now we're getting somewhere! Dr. Clayton will know if Barbara Hostetler was indeed carrying triplets."

"I don't think so. Barbara left Dr. Pierce for Dr. Bauer months ago. Besides, there's been a lot of new patients since then."

"But it wouldn't hurt to try, would it? Would you happen to know his number offhand?"

"I do, but it won't do you any good."

I stared. "How did you know I'm having a hard time with phones?"

She shrugged. "I just know that Dr. Clayton can't be reached."

"He's on vacation too?"

"He's in Haiti, doing volunteer work for his church. He does that every summer."

"They don't have phones in Haiti?" If Hernia had phones, I just assumed the rest of the world did.

"Some people have telephones, but not in the mountain village he visits. Last year Dr. Pierce tried to call him about a case, and he ended up sending a telegram that took six days to get there. One of the permanent missionaries mailed it to Dr. Clayton after he returned."

"Why, this is ridiculous!" I said it so loud both Patches and Tiddlywinks leaped from their places, their tails inflated. Ming, however, remained dangerously close to my head.

"Dr. Clayton is a very dedicated man," she said evenly. "He donates his services. Other doctors spend their vacations on golf courses. Dr. Clayton delivers babies for the poor. He's not a Mennonite, you know, but he is a kind and generous man. And so gentle. It's a pleasure just to work next door to him."

That sounded like more than hero worship to me. Perhaps the chaste Miss Mast was carrying a torch for the medical missionary. That wouldn't be the first time a mature Mennonite woman had been beguiled by a man in authority. Mama went absolutely nuts when Reverend Kurtz became Beechy Grove Mennonite Church's youngest pastor ever. Reverend Kurtz was a bachelor, and Mama baked him a pie, cake, or some other sweet every day of his short stay among us. Little did Mama know that Reverend Kurtz was a diabetic with absolutely no willpower. I'm not saying that Mama killed the preacher, but if she had baked those pies for Papa—who had no dietary problems—Reverend Kurtz might have stuck around long enough to marry me, and my parents would have gotten along a whole lot better.

"Is Dr. Clayton married?" I asked gently.

Tears flowed from the green eyes. "But his wife is such a mean woman. We have joint Christmas parties, you see, and he doesn't even look at the nurses. But she always glares at him. He deserves much better."

"Like you?"

She nodded. "I'd make him a good wife. I know I would."

"He's not a Mennonite, dear. You just said so yourself."

"But he's a lay missionary."

"Which denomination is he?"

"Presbyterian."

I gasped. "My sister Susannah married one of those. The next thing I knew she was painting her toenails and watching television. Once, when she thought she was alone, I even caught her"—I blushed—"I can't say it. It's just too embarrassing."

"Shaving her legs?" she asked in an awed whisper.

"Yes." I hung my head in shame. "All that good God-given insulation literally down the drain."

"Well, I wouldn't go that far!"

"All the same, you don't want to set your prayer cap for a married man. It will just end in heartbreak. Trust me, I know."

She blew her nose loudly. "That's right. I'd forgotten. You're the bigamist from Beechy Grove Mennonite Church."

"An inadvertent bigamist," I wailed.

"We at First Mennonite Church were scandalized—well, I wasn't. I'm a nurse, after all. I've seen everything." Her jaw tilted defiantly. "I would even shave my underarms for the right man."

I gasped in awe. "What if he doesn't like cats?"

She stiffened. "Do you think that's possible?"

"Face it, dear, even a cat lover isn't going to necessarily welcome thirty-two cats. Would you be willing to give up even one of these precious dears for a man? They're barely litter-trained themselves, you know. Always leaving the toilet seat up like that, or forgetting to put the top seat down. Why, I read somewhere that a small cat can easily drown in a toilet bowl. Kittens do all the time."

Her face had turned the color of powdered sugar. "Men!" she rasped.

"Men!" I said.

"Meow!" Ming howled.

I stood. "It's been really nice talking to you, Melba."

"You too, Magdalena. I wish I could have helped you more."

"Are you sure you can't tell me the names of those other two patients?"

Her eyes flickered.

"It could be a matter of life and death," I coaxed.

"What if I just gave you hints?"

"Hint away!"

"They both work at Miller's Feed Store here in Hernia—well, the Amish girl used to. I don't think she does anymore."

"Thank you." I reached for her hand and pumped it. I would have hugged Melba, but I didn't want to give a woman with thirty-two cats the wrong idea—her lust for Dr. Clayton aside. Besides, she was covered with enough cat hair to knit a small sweater. It was bad enough that my bottom looked like something the cat dragged in.

"You'll come back to visit sometime, won't you? The puddy-tats would wov dat, wouldn't dey?" She cooed in Ming's face. Ming flattened himself against the wall and hissed.

"Well—"

"You know, it's remarkable, but just this morning I was thinking about organizing a singles club for the over-forties crowd."

"That sounds like fun. I'll see if my new boyfriend wants to join."

She swallowed. "Actually, I was thinking more of a support group for women who'd never been proposed to."

"Sort of a Spinsters Anonymous?"

Melba frowned. "Spinsters is such an ugly word. I was thinking more of the Never Been Asked. We'd call ourselves the NBA for short."

"That is such an interesting idea," I said, and edged out the door. "You do realize, don't you, that I wouldn't qualify? Aaron may have been the slime on the sludge that sticks to the muck at the bottom of the pond, but he did ask me to marry him. He even gave me a ring."

Melba smiled. "I'd be willing to make an exception in your case."

"Thanks for everything," I said, and sprinted to my car.

Nine

I dreaded going to Miller's Feed Store. Elspeth Miller hates me.

Roy Miller, Elspeth's husband, is a triple fifth cousin of mine, but I certainly don't claim him. The official rumor has it that Roy beats Elspeth. Some of us, however, believe that it is Elspeth Rhinehart Miller who beats up on Roy. Elspeth is a German-German, not a Swiss-German like most of the Mennonites and Amish in the Hernia area. What's more, she was baptized a Lutheran—as an *infant* no less! No Mennonite or Amishman can comprehend such a senseless act. Perhaps it was being splashed with all that water as a tiny baby that put Elspeth in such a foul mood.

One might have more respect for Roy if he didn't allow Elspeth to push him around. A man *should* listen to his wife (didn't Papa?), but he shouldn't put up with hitting. No one should—not even a true pacifist like Roy. Sadly, the long-sleeved shirts that Roy habitually wears, even on the hottest days, are not a sign of his Mennonite modesty. What makes the whole thing seem even sadder is that Elspeth is a little bitty thing with a beaked nose and horn-rimmed glasses that flare out like butterfly wings. She seems about as dangerous as a swallowtail.

The Millers sell feed and farm equipment to Amish, Mennonite, and other farmers in the area. In addition, they also sell hard-to-find items like corrugated washboards and hand-operated ringers. There are also some "fancy" goods like blue-enameled cookware, black felt hats, bonnets, and even candy. Think of Miller's Feed Store as an Amish Wal-Mart. It is, incidentally, Hernia's largest employer.

But back to why Elspeth hates me. I can only guess it is because I have, upon occasion, stuck up for Roy. I do *not,* however, as Elspeth asserts, have "a ting for my man."

Nonetheless, I tried to slip into the store unnoticed and headed straight for Roy, who was demonstrating a nifty little gadget that peeled, cored, and sliced an apple in a matter of seconds. Several Amish women were watching, wide-eyed.

"We can make good *snitz* with that," said one.

"Dried apple slices," another said, needlessly translating for me.

Roy saw me and handed the machine to the nearest shopper. "You can buy a cheaper one in Bedford," he said, "but it won't be as good."

The women nodded. Roy had a reputation for telling the truth.

"Magdalena," he said, and grabbing one of my elbows, steered me down a narrow aisle. Galvanized buckets of all sizes hung on one side, horse bridals and currycombs on the other. Satisfied we were alone, Roy released me. "You shouldn't have come. Elspeth's working today."

"Then she'll just have to get over it. This is a free country, and I can shop anywhere I please."

"Please make it Bedford. You know what happened the last time she saw you."

"I did *not* knock down that display of lantern globes. She did. And frankly, it's stupid to stack glass like that."

"I couldn't agree more, but it was her idea." Roy lowered his voice. "She better not see you today, Magdalena. She's been on the warpath since she woke up. So, could you just buy what you came to buy, and then get out?"

I tried not to even glance at Roy's arms, but it was no use. He was wearing long sleeves again. It was stifling in the store, so it had to be because he had something to hide. Although in all fairness, I suppose they could have been old bruises.

"Sorry, but I didn't come to buy, dear. I need information."

Roy looked like a deer caught in my headlights. "What kind of information? You're not on your Nazi kick again, are you, Magdalena? Elspeth was born after the war, and she's been in the U.S. since she was sixteen."

"This has nothing to do with the Fuehrer and his flunkies. I need information about two of your employees who are in the family way."

"Ach!" Roy squawked, reverting to his ancestral ways. "You're not here to try and form a union, are you?"

I smiled. "Don't be ridiculous, dear. I don't work here, remember? I just want to talk to these ladies."

Roy glanced both ways. "What about?"

"Baby clothes," I said, thinking fast on my feet. When you wear size eleven like I do, it's really not that hard. And yes, I know it's wrong to lie, but fibbing to placate Freni is not so much a lie as a means of survival. The Bible says nothing against trying to save one's own life.

"What about baby clothes?"

"Well, Barbara Hostetler, whom you know to be a dear friend and distant cousin of mine—probably yours too—just had twins and—"

"Congratulations!" Roy was sincere.

"I'll tell her that. Anyway, as you may know, baby clothes are very expensive, so I got to thinking about sort of a joint shower—well, really, it's a woman thing. Just tell me where I can find the two ladies in question, let me chat to them a little, and I'll skeedaddle."

Roy shook his head. "Rebecca Zook no longer works here. And Mandilla Gindlesperger is on maternity leave, starting today. That's all I'm at liberty to say."

That was all the information I needed to know right then. Zook was a solid Amish name, that family having come over in the first major immigration in the eighteenth century. Both Freni and I had Zook branches in our family trees. Freni often shopped at Miller's Feed Store and undoubtedly knew the family, possibly even where Rebecca lived. And it just so happened that I knew Mandilla Gindlesperger.

Mandilla and I went to school together, kindergarten through twelfth grade. Only back then she was Mandilla Beechy. It was, in fact, her great-great-grandfather, Bishop Beechy, who split off from the Amish and founded Beechy Grove Mennonite Church. Because of this suspicious family connection, Mandilla always thought she was better than the rest of us—well, at least better than I. Always big for her age, Mandilla would push me off the monkey bars, stop me on the slide, stick gum in my hair, and—this was her favorite way to torment me—sit on my paper lunch sack. That was, of course, in grammar school. In high school, Mandilla began to act a little nicer, quiet even. By our senior year Mandilla was an overweight, introspective woman who sometimes cried in study hall.

I thanked Roy for the tip. "I didn't even know Mandilla was pregnant again. Isn't she a little old for that kind of thing?"

Before Roy could answer I was hit on the behind by a mighty force and knocked off my feet. Fortunately Roy has quick reflexes and was able to catch me.

"Get out of my husband's arms!" Elspeth shrieked.

I struggled to stand, but was hit again.

"Elspeth, *please,*" I heard Roy say meekly.

Sheer anger got me upright and facing my attacker. Elspeth Miller had a look of pure hate in her eyes. In her tiny, gnarled hands, she held a coal shovel.

"Get out of my store, you hussy," she hissed.

"What did you say?"

"You heard what I said, you two-bit trollop." For a foreigner, Elspeth's command of English is remarkable. "And don't try playing Miss Innocent with me, Magdalena Yoder. You forget that Roy is Aaron Miller's first cousin. We know all about how you seduced that poor man, and then turned on him when you learned that he was broke."

I gasped, depleting the large store of half its oxygen. "That's not what happened! Aaron seduced *me.* And he was already married. Why didn't any of you Millers tell me that? I went to my marriage bed a virgin," I wailed, "only it wasn't my marriage bed at all, but a den of iniquity. You all stood back and watched me be led like a lamb to the slaughter."

Elspeth raised the shovel, this time over her head. "Lies," she said. "It's all lies. And now you're trying to get your hands on my Roy. Well, I won't have it!"

I took a wary step back, away from the shovel, but in doing so, moved closer to Roy.

"I said to get away from him!" Elspeth snarled, and despite her tiny size, brought the shovel down with a force hard enough to stun a bull.

Now, I may be lanky, but I'm also fairly nimble, and managed to step aside. Unfortunately, Roy Miller has two left feet (I mean that literally—thanks to an insufficient gene pool). The shovel scoop that was meant for my noggin connected with Roy's, and he folded like an accordion.

"Now see what you've done!" Elspeth shrieked.

"Me?"

She threw down the shovel, dropped to her knees, and cradled her husband's head. "You've killed my Roy!"

I glanced around. A crowd was forming at either end of the aisle. I had a choice: defend myself, or do something for Roy.

"Call 911," I said to the mostly Amish crowd.

No one moved.

"Call the police!" Elspeth barked.

Alas, someone did.

I never used to understand how a man with a brain the size of a flea's was able to become police chief in my fair town. That he has managed to stay chief so long was beyond my comprehension. But I have given the matter a good deal of thought, and have at last

concluded that the Good Lord created Melvin Stoltzfus as my personal nemesis. Melvin is my cross to
bear, the means by which I am tested. Through my
encounters with that irritating arthropod I am expected to grow stronger, perhaps even to learn to love
my fellow man. I am, I confess, a slow learner in
this regard.

The police station is less than a mile from the feed
store, and Melvin should have been able to get there
in a minute or two. But that was not the case. Perhaps
the man had his shoes untied, and couldn't find anyone to tie them, or maybe he misplaced the map that
showed the way to the front door of the police station.
At any rate, it took Melvin a good fifteen minutes to
show, and by then I could hear the approaching wail
of Hernia's only ambulance. Someone, thank heavens,
had called for real help after all.

I am pleased to report that Roy Miller was not seriously injured. By the time help arrived, he was on his
feet—albeit somewhat unsteadily—and although the
medics insisted that he accompany them back to the
hospital, he was released an hour later. In fact, Elspeth
didn't even bother to accompany him, but remained
behind to keep the store open.

In the meantime, Melvin predictably made my life
miserable. No sooner had Roy been whisked away
than my new brother-in-law turned on me.

"Yoder, I want you to come with me down to the
station."

I glanced around. There were still people four deep
at the ends of the aisle. Elspeth was among them, no
doubt eager to see me arrested.

"Don't be ridiculous, dear. You know it was Elspeth
who conked him on the head, not me."

"Did not!" Elspeth called from the sidelines.

I may have stuck my tongue out at her.

"Yoder, don't make a scene."

"I'm not making a scene, you are."

"Yoder!" The man is ten years younger than me, but has the nerve to speak to me like I'm a fourth-grade girl, and he's my teacher, Miss Enz.

"Leave me alone, Melvin. Go back to work, or better yet, go home and let your wife devour you."

"What's that supposed to mean?"

"Isn't that what happens to male praying mantises?"

"Very funny, Yoder." Melvin Stoltzfus knew exactly what I meant. I know we can't help how we look (if we could, would I look like Trigger on steroids?), but Melvin looks exactly like a five-foot eight-inch praying mantis, give or take a tentacle.

"Just leave me alone, Melvin. I've had a long, hard day."

Melvin fumbled with a pair of handcuffs that dangled from his side. "Yoder, I have to talk to you, and you're not making this easy."

"I have no intention of making it easy, Melvin, I know my rights."

"Then I'm afraid I'm going to have to arrest you."

"On what grounds?"

"Disturbing the peace."

"Arrest her, arrest her," Elspeth chanted. Much to my relief no one joined in.

"Melvin should arrest *you,* dear. You're the one who habitually beats up on your husband."

"Slander!" Elspeth cried. "Did everyone hear that?"

One or two people nodded, but nobody said anything. There was a lot of staring going on, however, and not all of it from the crowd.

Melvin's eyes do not function as a pair, and he had one trained on Elspeth, the other on me. "Maybe we could find someplace here to talk," he said.

"I have nothing to say that I haven't already said. Just the same, I'll say it one more time. I did *not* hit Roy over the head with that shovel."

"It isn't about Roy," Melvin said, his voice barely audible. "It's about your sister."

"Susannah?" What a silly way for me to respond. I only have one sister—that I know of.

Both of Melvin's orbs focused briefly on Elspeth. "Is there somewhere I could interview this woman? Maybe a storeroom?"

Much to my surprise, Elspeth grinned. "The unloading door is locked now. She won't be able to get away if I lock you in from this side."

"That won't be necessary," Melvin said, even more to my surprise.

Elspeth frowned but led us through the throng, and eventually through a set of scuffed metal doors at the far end of the store. Just inside the storeroom she grabbed a pitchfork from a barrel and handed it to Melvin.

"If she tries to get away, just poke."

"In your eye," I said, forgetting for a moment that, as a Christian, I'm supposed to keep a civil tongue.

"Ladies, please," Melvin said. That was quite possibly the first time he had ever used the P word on me.

Elspeth drew another fork from the barrel. "Don't worry. I'll be waiting just on the other side of those doors. She won't get away."

I glared at Elspeth. "What's with the forks and shovels? Don't you usually ride a broom?"

Melvin snickered. I had the feeling he disliked her almost as much as he disliked me.

"Why I never!" Elspeth said, and stormed off, fork still in hand.

I prayed silently for her customers on the other side of the door. I also waited until the doors had swung shut behind her before speaking, and you can be sure that when I did, it was in a whisper.

"Now, what's this about Susannah?"

Melvin sat on an empty wooden crate turned sideways. He sighed dramatically.

"Out with it," I snapped.

"Remember those little fried apple pies your mama used to make?"

"Snitz turnovers? The ones with dried apples."

"Yeah, those are the ones. Susannah's making them."

"*What?* She hates to cook!" I'm not sure my slothful sister knows what a stove looks like anymore.

"And that's not all. She bought a dress."

"A *dress*?" To my knowledge Susannah hasn't worn a dress since our parents' funeral eleven years ago. She hasn't worn pants either since then. Don't get me wrong. She doesn't go around naked, like that vamp Vivian and her boy-toy. To the contrary, my baby sister drapes herself in yards of fabric, and floats through the house like the ghost of a half-wrapped mummy.

"It gets worse."

I steadied myself against a stack of heavy barley bags. "Go on."

"She's stopped wearing makeup."

I gasped, thereafter choking for a few seconds on barley dust. *"None?"*

"Not a lick. I didn't recognize her at first. She

looked awful. In fact, Yoder, I thought it was you come to pay a visit."

"Thanks, dear." I would have pinched Melvin, had my knees been strong enough to get me that close.

"Oh, I'm not through yet, Yoder. We're just getting to the good parts."

I slumped to the floor. "I don't know if my ticker can take any more."

Melvin leaned forward, no doubt checking for a shadow under the swinging metal doors. "This morning she made the bed."

"Lies, Melvin, those have got to be communist lies!"

Melvin is linguistically challenged. "Now this is the piece of resistance," he said, and proceeded to tell me the most shocking thing these ears have ever heard, bar none. If there had been anyone else present to revive me except for Melvin, I would have fainted.

Ten

Easy Snitz Turnovers*

✦

2 cups dried apple slices
½ cup sugar
2 tablespoons butter
1 teaspoon cinnamon
¼ teaspoon nutmeg
2 nine-inch pie crusts cut in half

Soak dried apples in two cups warm water. Cook until tender. Drain off most of the liquid, and stir in sugar, butter, cinnamon, and nutmeg. Divide pie crust into halves. Spoon several tablespoons of apples on one-half of each pie crust half. Fold over, moisten edges, and crimp.

Fry in deep fat at 375 degrees for approximately four minutes or until golden brown. If baking, bake in oven at 375 degrees for approximately twenty minutes.

Yields four large turnovers.

*If my slothful, slovenly sister can make these, anyone can.

Eleven

"**S**he what?" I asked weakly.

"Your sister asked me to take her to church next Sunday."

I fanned myself with my skirt. Of course it was an immodest thing to do, but Melvin politely averted at least one eye.

"Did you say *church*?"

"Yeah, Yoder. Did you put her up to this?"

"Don't be ridiculous. Susannah hasn't listened to me since she hit puberty. I wonder what those pushy Presbyterians are bribing her with now."

"That's just it, Yoder. She doesn't want to go to the Presbyterian church, she wants to go back to the Mennonite church. Beechy Grove Mennonite to be exact."

I know, by now you must be wondering why it is I wasn't rejoicing. I'll tell you why. The Susannah that Melvin had just described was not my sister. Or if it was, she was deathly ill.

"Shnookums!" I cried. "Does she still have Shnookums?"

Melvin shrugged. "I haven't seen that mutt around for ages."

I felt a sharp pang in my heart. Something was

dreadfully wrong. Susannah and her pitiful pooch are inseparable. Who else would carry a dinky dog around in her bra? She even has that miserable mongrel trained to brush her teeth. That's right—the *dog* brushes Susannah's teeth.

"What shall we do, Melvin?" My voice sounded like a little girl who'd been sucking on her helium balloon.

Tears rolled out of Melvin's left eye. "I don't know, Yoder. That's why I came to you."

I closed my eyes and prayed. I asked the Good Lord for strength, wisdom, and, above all, patience. Now that I've conquered pride, a lack of patience is my one shortcoming. At any rate, after praying for a few minutes I felt calm, collected, and as my former guests from Hollywood might have said, "centered." I knew exactly what I needed to do, and much to my amazement, I didn't even have to struggle to get to my feet.

"Where are you going, Yoder?"

"To see your wife!"

"Good luck." He was actually sincere.

"Thanks, but I won't be needing luck. I'm a woman on a divine mission."

I strode from the storeroom, through the swinging metal doors, and straight into the tines of Elspeth's pitchfork.

"Ouch!"

Fortunately for me, Elspeth was engaged in a conversation with a customer, and her grip on the fork was loose. Unfortunately for Elspeth, my bony elbow knocked the fork out of her hand, and true to its name, it pitched. The heavy scoop brought the tines down on the tip of Elspeth's black brogan, while the handle swung up, hitting her chin.

Elspeth screamed bloody murder, all the while hopping about like a one-legged chicken on a hot asphalt road. For a heart-stopping moment I thought I may have done her serious harm.

"Call 911 again," I wailed miserably.

The Amish woman Elspeth had been talking to stared at me, her eyes as big as snitz turnovers.

"Never mind, I'll do it myself."

But before I could move, the swinging metal doors parted and Melvin burst on the scene. Alas, he didn't seem at all surprised.

"What did you do this time, Yoder?"

"*Me?* I didn't do anything."

Elspeth froze in mid-hop. "Magdalena tried to kill me, that's what she did. Look!" She pointed first to her chin, which sprouted a nice little tuft of hair, but no bruise as far as I could see. "And there!" Elspeth, who was really quite agile for a woman her age, grabbed her right foot and raised it almost chest level.

I, for one, tried to focus on Elspeth's foot, and not her unmentionables which, incidentally, could stand a good bleaching. To be honest, there was a small indentation in the leather of her shoe, just above the spot where her big toe should be, but it was really nothing to get upset about.

"A little shoe polish, and who's going to notice the difference?" I said in a reassuring voice.

"Arrest that woman!" Elspeth screeched. Balancing on one bandy leg, she unlaced her brogan, removed it and the sock, and searched in vain for a wound.

I was shocked by the state of Elspeth's foot. "You really should trim your nails, dear."

"Your foot looks all right to me," Melvin said, obviously much relieved. Even a man with half a brain would want to stay clear of a fight between Elspeth and me.

"But she tried to kill me!"

"Nonsense, dear," I said calmly. "You were the one holding the weapon. Anna," I said to our Amish witness, "you saw it happen. It was an accident, wasn't it?"

"Ach!" Anna squawked and fled from the store.

"You see? She doesn't even think answering the question is worth her time. Well, I've got to go too." I trotted after Anna, fully expecting to be tackled by Elspeth.

Much to my surprise, she made no move to stop me.

Melvin and Susannah live in a modest, aluminum-sided home on the south end of Hernia. This is a new neighborhood of blue-collar folks, and bears the lofty, but nonsensical name Foxcroft. In my dictionary a croft is either a small, enclosed field adjoining a house, or a small farm worked by tenants. It has nothing to do with rows of identical homes on postage-stamp lots.

Since all the homes on Susannah's street, Fox*haven,* look the same, and all the unimaginatively planted yards are in their infancy, I was forced to pay attention to house numbers. Unfortunately for me, the builder of this subdivision bought his numerals from the same company that supplies the last line of letters on eye charts. Fortunately, however, Susannah's blinds were open, and on my third pass I noticed the hot pink drapes. I never did see the 666 that was supposedly tacked to the right of the front door.

As it was already well into the afternoon, I was pretty sure I would catch my sister awake. And no, she doesn't hold down a night job. Susannah and daylight have just never really gotten along. Maybe it is because she was born at night. Who knows? But even as a baby Susannah kept midnight hours.

Frankly, I think sleeping past eight in the morning is a sin. The Good Lord created sunrise and sunset to tell us when to get up, and when to go to bed, respectively. Not the other way around. And for those of us who strive for holiness, he created roosters. My cock Chauntecleer, for example, crows every morning at five thirty-five. Smarter than most humans, he even knows how to adjust for daylight savings time. This is not to say that I get up with the chickens, however. Chauntecleer has been repeatedly warned to keep the racket down before six, or one of these days he's going to end up as a fricassee.

Susannah opened the door before I even had a chance to ring the bell. Had I been wearing dentures, I would have dropped them on the porch.

"Oh, silly, stop your staring," Susannah said, after perhaps five minutes had passed.

How could I not stare? My baby sister did indeed own a dress now, and she was wearing it: a modest, short-sleeved navy shirtdress with a white collar. It was buttoned at the throat. Susannah's knees were covered by the skirt, but her legs were encased in hose. On her feet she had proper, store-bought shoes. They weren't even patent leather.

"Uh—uh—"

Susannah pulled me inside. "Do I look that bad?"

I shook my head.

"So you approve?"

"Well—"

Susannah pushed me into an armchair. "You look like you've seen a ghost, Mags."

"It is quite a shock. You always wore jeans as a girl, and then those—how shall we say—flowing outfits. I hadn't seen your legs in so many years, I wasn't sure if I remembered correctly. But I see now that you were indeed born with ankles."

"Very funny, Mags. You hate it, don't you?"

"Let's just say it isn't you."

"But it *is* me. It's the new me."

I glanced around at an impeccably clean house—and yes, I could see most of the house from that one little room. It would take a dorm full of college kids an entire week to turn it into a replica of Susannah's old room at home.

"Why?" I asked quietly.

She was still standing, and I could see for the first time that she had a figure. Not a curvaceous one—you can't have that *and* wear a dog in your bra, but a decent enough form nonetheless. If I, her sister, looked anywhere near that good, I was, in her words, "one hot mama."

Susannah shook her head, and I noticed that even her hair was neatly combed and held in place with a veneer of spray. "Isn't this what you guys wanted?"

"We guys who?"

"You, Melvin, the whole world!"

I was flabbergasted. "You threw away your bandage dresses for us?"

Susannah sighed. "They weren't bandage dresses, Mags, but yes, I threw them away."

"I repeat. Why?"

To my astonishment, she burst into tears. "Because I'm married now, that's why!"

"What does that have to do with anything?"

Susannah threw herself on the Berber carpet at my

feet. "I'm supposed to be normal now. Don't you get it? Look out there!" She pointed past the hot pink drapes. In the driveway across the street I could see a woman about Susannah's age washing her car clad only in halter top and shorts.

"She isn't dressed like you, dear."

"Yes, but she isn't the police chief's wife."

My mousy brown hair bristled. "So that's what it's about, is it? Melvin asked you to dress like this? Like Barbie goes to church?"

"Oh, no! Melvin didn't ask me to do anything. I want to do this for him. For his career."

I tried not to smile. "Susannah, dear, I'm afraid he's gotten as far as he's going to go, and he did it all unmarried, and while dating you, Queen of the Fabric Outlet Mall."

"Mags, you are so wrong. Melvin is going places. Hernia is just his jumping-off place."

"Too bad we don't have any really high cliffs," I mumbled.

"I know you've never liked him, but he has so much potential. Someday he may decide to run for the state legislature, maybe even the national. Who knows, maybe someday there will be a Stoltzfus in the White House."

I shuddered. Well, at least the nation wasn't unprepared.

"What about church, dear? Is that why you want to go to church? To get the Religious Right to back you?"

Susannah looked away. "Yeah, that and other things."

"What other things?"

She was silent for a long time, and I respected that until I saw tears.

"Susannah, tell me," I said gently.

"I want to stop being a disappointment. To you—and to Mama and Papa."

That caught me off guard. "Me?"

She turned a tear-streaked face my way. "I want you to respect me, Mags."

"I do." Okay, so it was a fib, but the Good Lord knows I tell only necessary lies.

"No, you don't. You think I'm a floozy."

"Not anymore, dear. Now you're just a former floozy." I laughed at my little joke. "But seriously, Susannah, this isn't you, is it?"

She glanced at me, then away. "Well, I no longer sleep around, if that's what you mean."

"Good. Sleeping around is dangerous under any circumstances. But I mean this—" I waved at her clothes and the neat surroundings. "Except for those hot pink drapes, this could be anybody's house. Anybody boring."

"I bought the drapes before I began my transformation. I had them custom-made. I can't take them back."

"I don't think you should. They are very you."

"You want me to be myself?"

"Perhaps you could compromise. Perhaps—oh, forget what I just said. Yes, you should be yourself."

"Really?"

"Really. Wear your drapes if you like. Swaddle yourself in enough fabric to clothe a third world country for all I care. I just want you to be happy, and you don't look very happy now."

She beamed, but a second later her face darkened. "What about Melvin?"

I was tempted to tell her to forget about the miserable mantis, that his opinion didn't count. But it did. And anyway, there was no need for her to worry any longer.

"The man worships you. Of course worshipping a human being is a sin, but that's another issue. My point is, he loves *you*. And we all know this isn't you. As for the voters—well, they'll vote anything into office that promises them financial stability. Promise them a Porsche in every pot, so to speak. Go for it, girl!"

Susannah yelped with joy, grabbed my hands, and pulled me to my feet. Then in an act that defied five hundred years of stern Anabaptist inbreeding, she enveloped me in a hug. Disregarding my own, almost identical set of genes, I hugged her back.

A second later I screamed.

Twelve

"**O**uch! He bit my bosom!"

Susannah patted the left side of her own bosom. "You mean Shnookums?"

"That mangy, miserable, maniacal mutt bit me!"

"Aw, Mags, he's just happy to see you."

"Well, I didn't see him! In fact, dressed the way you are, in a *real* dress, I just assumed that he was living on the ground now like any normal animal."

Susannah recoiled in horror. "Shnookums is not an animal!"

"He's a dog, dear. And that's if you're being charitable. I've seen rats in Philly twice his size and every bit as nice."

"But they're not housebroken, are they?" She sounded almost hopeful, like she was considering a Philadelphia rat to balance the load.

"Aren't you even a little concerned that I might be hurt?"

"Well, are you?"

I peered down my dress at my deficit chest. There didn't appear to be any teeth marks. Maybe I ought to have given the rat credit for finding the needle in a haystack.

"I guess I'll live. But you better teach that beast some manners."

"You squeezed him, Mags. What was he supposed to do?"

"You hugged me first," I said childishly. My behavior raised a sobering thought. "It's a good thing you don't have little kids, and by the time you do, well—*it* may no longer be around by then."

"Actually we've been trying to start a family ever since we knew for sure we were getting married."

"You *have*?" The thought of being an aunt delighted me. The thought of a possible little Melvin running around terrified me.

Susannah nodded. "Melvin wants a big family, and I'm already thirty-five. It's now or never, as they say."

"You could adopt," I wailed.

"Don't be silly, Mags. We'll do that too. Like I said, Melvin wants to have a bunch of kids."

"How much is a bunch?" I asked in alarm.

"Oh, at least a dozen. Six adopted, and six with my honeybuns."

Before I could stop them, images of miniature mantises flitted through my brain.

"Six mini Melvins isn't a bunch," I cried. "It's a *swarm*!"

The doorbell rang. Susannah kicked off her shoes before running to answer it, proving that old habits do indeed die hard. No doubt, by the time I left, she'd be back in her swaddling clothes.

"Hemmy!" I heard her say.

I heard a familiar voice, but not wanting to be rude, ignored the caller and studied my sister's decor. Granted, Melvin makes a meager salary, and Susannah none, but their tiny house was crammed with expensive furnishings. An enormous, buttery soft Italian leather sofa took up one entire living-room wall. In front of it were two buttery soft ottomans and a cherry coffee table around which a family of five could eat a full-course meal. Above the couch hung a signed, limited edition print by Jim Booth, the famous landscape painter. Opposite the couch was the largest TV screen I had ever seen. The devil himself could, and probably did, appear life-size on that thing. Against the far wall, between the oversized TV and decadent leather sofa, loomed a monstrous electronic exercise machine that looked like a cross between a bicycle and a medieval instrument of torture—the Exorcisist, Susannah once called it—which tells you more about yourself than you'll ever want to know. How's that for priorities? Young people these days!

I know for a fact that Susannah and her hopeless hubby are up to their eyeballs in credit card debt. In my day we saved up our money until we had enough, and then we paid cash. Okay, so I inherited an inn full of antique furniture—the real thing too, none of those faux, factory-distressed things they sell nowadays. Who wants to pay good money for a table or chair with pretend scars? If I'm going to dish out that much money, I want a new table that I can scar for myself. At any rate, I have always made do with what I had, or made more dough to do *with*. I have never, and will never, own a single credit card.

In case you're wondering why I inherited all my parents' furniture—well, I didn't. Papa and Mama, in their wisdom, left the farm and its contents to me, with the provision that I share equally with my sister when I saw that she was responsible enough not to squander her inheritance. The farm, and by extension the PennDutch, is still under my control. However, when Susannah got married the *first* time, I made the terrible mistake of giving her not only half of our parents' genuinely distressed furniture, but first pick. Fortunately my sister thought veneer was a disease and inlay the act which caused it. She picked the most modern pieces and then promptly turned around and sold them to get money for a king-size waterbed and a beanbag living-room suite.

Ten years later this still annoys me, and I was clucking to myself when Susannah got my attention.

"Mags, I want you to meet my new neighbor. Her name is Gizella Hemingway."

I stared at her visitor. There was no doubt about it. That was Gizella Hemingway all right. *Nurse* Gizella Hemingway.

"It's you!" Nurse Hemingway humphed.

I was more polite and extended my hand. "What a surprise, dear."

Nurse Hemingway handed me what may just as well have been a wet dishrag. "I didn't know you two were sisters. I mean, I noticed the resemblance, but I thought maybe you were Susannah's mother."

I wrung the dishrag until its owner winced. I have been told that I have a strong grip. Well, if that's so, it comes from pinching pennies like the Good Lord intended us to do.

"You thought I was *Barbara's* mother," I said evenly. "And Jonathan's. Well, I'm nobody's mother. I'm certainly not old enough to be either of their mothers."

"Looks can be deceiving," Nurse Hemingway said. I eyeballed her bleached blond hair with the high contrast roots. "Some of us are not so easily deceived."

"What's that supposed to mean?"

"Never mind."

Meanwhile, Susannah was staring at us the way I stared at Aaron on my wedding night. "Do you two know each other?"

"We met at the hospital, dear. I meant to tell you, Barbara's had her babies."

Susannah shrieked with joy and jumped up and down. I don't know if it was the joy or the jumping, but something set the crazy canine off, and he began to howl like a banshee.

"Triplets!" Susannah trilled. "I'm an aunt to triplets."

"Aoooooooooooooo," Shnookums shrilled. "Aoooooooooooooo." I can't translate exactly for the mutt, but he pretty much agreed with Susannah. He may, however, have referred to himself as an uncle.

"Actually, dear," I said to my sister, "you're only a kissing cousin several times removed. And you," I said to the pea-brained pooch, "aren't even in the family tree. Besides, Barbara didn't have triplets after all. Only twins."

Susannah stopped jumping. *"What?"*

"Ask your friend Hemorrhoid here. She was there."

"That's Hemmy," the bottle blonde snapped, "and only my friends get to call me that."

Susannah grabbed Nurse Hemingway by an arm. "What's this about there being only twins? I was supposed to be auntie to three Hostetler babies."

"Kissing cousin!" I hissed.

Both women ignored me. "Apparently Mrs. Hostetler's OB-GYN was mistaken. Doctor's are human, you know.''

Susannah is a smart girl. She stopped believing in Santa Claus after seeing two of them on the streets of Bedford last year. For her, seeing is believing.

"But you were there, Hemmy, right? You helped deliver the babies, right?"

"I did. There were only two."

"I can't believe this!" Susannah wailed, and buried her face in hands that are long and beautiful, very much like my own.

Nurse Hemingway shook her barely blond head. "I don't get it. Mrs. Hostetler delivered two beautiful, perfectly healthy boys this morning, and by the way you people have been acting, you'd think there was a death in the family."

I sighed. There was, I suppose, no need to kill the messenger. So what if this messenger had dark roots and was an immigrant from Pittsburgh? Some of the nicest people in the world live there, and even on the Magdalena Scale of Sin (transgressions that aren't covered by the Bible, but should be) dyeing one's hair rates only a nine.

"She was hoping for a namesake," I said. "So was Freni Hostetler, the grandmother."

"I still don't get it."

"Susannah, Freni, and I each want a baby named after us. This would have been a possibility if Barbara had delivered three girls. Barbara's mother is dead, you see, and we three are like—well, Susannah and I are like sisters to her. Okay, so maybe even that's an exaggeration in Susannah's case, but at least I'm like a sister to Barbara."

"And Mrs. Hostetler senior, this Freni woman, is like a mother to Barbara?"

"Not hardly. The two women can't stand each other. Still, one can always hope for a little namesake, can't one?"

Nurse Hemingway shrugged. "I was named Gizella after my grandmother. Gizella! In school, kids used to call me Godzilla. That's why I go by the nickname Hemmy."

"My middle name is Portulaca," I confessed. "Mama got the name from a seed catalogue."

"No kidding! Well, it's a good thing she didn't make Portulaca your first name. Magdalena—now, I like that. It's classy. Strong, but feminine. Distinctive without being bizarre. More people should name their babies Magdalena."

"Thank you. I couldn't agree more." I tried to think of something nice to say about her, but couldn't, so I resolved to keep my mouth tightly shut.

"What about my name?" Susannah whined. "What about Shnookum's name?"

"Yours is a beautiful name, dear," I said and patted her bare arm. I turned to Nurse Hemingway. "So, you're my sister's neighbor, are you?"

She nodded. "I'm renting the house next door, but I have an option to buy. I met Susannah my first day here. She was cutting her grass and—"

"Susannah was *mowing*?"

"Yes."

"In the daytime?"

"Of course."

I smiled reassuringly. "Don't worry, it won't happen again. We had a little sisterly chat, and things will be going back to normal now."

"I beg your pardon?"

"See that?" I said, pointing to Susannah, who had left our company and was busy taking down the drapes. "Give her ten minutes and a five-pound bucket of makeup—although putty will do in a pinch—and you won't recognize my sister."

"I don't understand."

"Just watch, dear."

We watched, she in horror, I in amusement, while my baby sister transformed from a prospective Mennonite church lady to Tammy Faye in bright pink bandages—either that or a dead geisha in a monochrome kimono. At any rate, Susannah has no shame and undressed and dressed right there in the living room.

"Oh, my goodness," Hemmy gasped, "what's that black hairy thing sticking out of her bra?"

"That's her dog, the infamous Shnookums."

At the sound of his name, the protruding pooch let out a plaintive howl. Still holding a grudge against the mutt, I howled back.

Nurse Hemingway's eyes widened. "My, what an interesting family you all are."

"Oh, it isn't just us, dear. We're typical Hernians. Or is it Herniatites? I can never get that right—oh!" I began to shimmy and shake like a heathen dancer. Maybe even a Presbyterian.

Nurse Hemingway stepped closer to me. "It isn't chest pains, is it?"

"Oh, no, dear. They're in my back, and they're really nothing to get excited about. It's just that my wings are beginning to emerge. They usually wait until later in the day."

Nurse Hemingway turned the color of Susannah's

foundation. "If you'll excuse me, I think I left the water running in my bathroom."

With that the transplanted Pittsburgher was out of there like an unrepentant sinner from a revival meeting.

"How could you do that, Mags?" Susannah demanded. She was now fully covered and made-up. Less than ten minutes had elapsed since the beginning of her metamorphosis.

"How could I do what, dear?" I asked innocently.

"Chase her away, that's what! Hemmy is my only friend."

"Don't be ridiculous, dear, you have lots of friends."

"Name one."

"Well, there's—uh—uh—there's me."

"*Besides* you."

"There's Melvin," I said reluctantly.

"And?"

"Freni and Barbara."

"They don't count. They only speak to me because I'm family, and they have to."

"Didn't you used to have a friend over in Somerset?" I asked hopefully.

"She's in solitary now, and they've revoked all her visiting privileges."

"Well, there's always that dinky dog of yours. He may as well be good for something."

"I meant human friends," she wailed, and then quickly whispered into the gap of fabric at her chest. "Sorry, Shnooky-wooky, Mama didn't mean to hurt your feelings."

"Aooo," Shnookums moaned. Apparently he was hurt.

I made a face at my sister's bosom. "Nurse Hemingway was hardly your friend if the sight of the real you sent her scurrying."

Susannah blinked at me. One advantage of such heavy makeup is that it discourages scowling.

"You must have said something nasty. What did you say, Mags?"

"Nothing nasty," I said, quite honestly. "Anyway, dear, you hardly knew this woman."

"I did so!"

"Tell me everything you know about her."

"Well, she's from New Jersey, she likes David Bowie's music, and she lies out in the sun just about every day."

I patted my sister's swaddled arm. "You see, dear, you don't know her that well after all. Nurse Hemingway is from Pittsburgh."

"No, she isn't. I saw the moving van. It had New Jersey plates."

"What about her car?"

Susannah shrugged. "I didn't pay attention to it. It's an old thing, and besides, *it* wasn't parked in my driveway."

"And her van was?"

"Just for a few minutes. The movers got the address wrong. Anyway, what difference does it make?"

"Maybe none." I glanced at my watch. It was far later than I had expected. In a little more than an hour my guests were going to expect supper on the table. The giggly gals from England and the ignoble Dr. Barnes had not been instructed to come up with a second meal. It was time to hustle my bustle home. "Hey," I said brightly, "gotta go, sis."

"You sure?" Susannah sounded disappointed, a fact

that pleased me. Maybe there was hope for us as sisters.

"Positive. *Tempus fugit.*" Alas, I may have mispronounced that noble Latin phrase.

Susannah gasped and then laughed. "Oh, Mags, I'm so proud of you. But if you're going to swear, at least get it right. It's—"

I clamped my hands over my ears and fled. Our bonding was going to have to happen in stages. There is only so much Susannah a good Christian can take in any twenty-four-hour period and still remain true to the faith.

Thirteen

It just so happened that if I turned left out of Fox-croft, and right on Blough Road and followed it back to town, I would pass within a block of Mandilla Gindlesperger's house. It would only take me a minute to stop and ask her a few questions. Then I could zip back up to the PennDutch, throw a can of soup on the stove, and give the hospital in Bedford a call to see how Mose was doing.

Unfortunately the Gindlespergers did not live in a nice part of town. Hernia is a fairly homogeneous town, but there are two small streets on the south side that are frequently, and uncharitably, referred to as Ragsdale. When Susannah and I were girls (at separate times, of course), our school bus used to stop in this part of town to take on students. It was common knowledge among us children that the Ragsdale kids were a breed apart. Some of them wore tattoos, many of them smoked, and on at least three occasions Miss Proschel, our bus driver, had to confiscate knives. Like many other stereotypes in this world, Ragsdale's bad reputation was based on both fact and fancy.

I will admit that I was nervous, when after leaving Susannah's brand-new and very bland burb, I headed toward Ragsdale. At the first sign of a broken-down sofa on the front porch, my pulse began to race. When I spotted the first washing machine beside one of those broken-down sofas, my heart began to pound. Call me prejudiced, but I just can't help it. I know that the depth of my feelings is irrational, but ever since Billy Scott sat on the bus beside me and demonstrated without a shadow of a doubt that he was too poor to wear underwear, I have been devoid of middle-class guilt.

The Gindlesperger house fits the Ragsdale profile perfectly. It was long and narrow with a gray, tarshingled exterior, and had a postage stamp-size yard. But it differed with the other houses on the street in that the yard was impeccably neat, and rows of lavender and white periwinkles lined the short, cracked walk. The front porch was devoid of both sofa and washing machine, sporting instead a wooden porch swing. The swing appeared to be homemade—and not a very good job at that—but in its own way, neat, and had been painted bright red.

The tidiness of the place did not surprise me. Levi and Mandilla Gindlesperger are both descended from long lines of Amish and Amish-Mennonites, all of pure ancestry. But somewhere along their road to heaven the Gindlespergers took a right turn and ended up worshiping at the First and Only True Church of the One and Only Living God of the Tabernacle of Supreme Holiness and Healing and Keeper of the Consecrated Righteousness of the Eternal Flame of Jehovah, a tiny, independent congregation up by the turnpike. Still, you might be able to take a Swiss person out of his or her religion, but you can't take order out of a Swiss. As long as they kept marrying cousins, the Gindlesperger descendants, no matter how poor they became, would continue to stand out in Ragsdale.

Although the front door was open, the house was protected by a neatly mended screen door. I peered through the screen before ringing the bell. The living room was dark and cool. The nearest piece of furniture was an orange and green plaid couch, its long straight back to the door.

I took a deep breath and rang the bell.

"Yes?" An enormous shape had risen from behind the wall of discordant plaid.

"Mandilla? Is that you?"

"Who are you?"

"Magdalena Yoder."

"Do I know you?"

"We went to high school together. I own the Penn-Dutch Inn now."

"Praise God," she said, and then, "just a minute."

It took more like five minutes for a very pregnant Mandilla Gindlesperger to hoist herself off the couch, waddle to the door, and flip the hook. She was out of breath.

"I was napping," she puffed. She was wearing a blue denim maternity smock over a white T-shirt. Her legs were bare, her feet clad in fuzzy, pink bunny slippers. Loose strands of mousy brown hair mocked the gold-tone clip at the back of her head.

"I'm sorry," I said quickly, "I didn't mean to wake you."

"I'm glad you did. It's a sin, but of course you know that."

"I beg your pardon?"

She motioned me in. "First Thessalonians, chapter five, verses six and seven. *'So then, let us not be like others, who are asleep, but let us be alert and self-controlled. For those who sleep, sleep at night.' "*

"Amen!" I said. It just so happened that I agreed. Susannah—well, the old Susannah, at any rate—thinks that all the numbers on the clock are P.M. Once, when she *had* to get up before noon to catch a bus, she asked to borrow an A.M. clock.

"Please sit," Mandilla said. She pointed to a ladderback chair that had had one of its rungs replaced with a yellow plastic rod, perhaps part of a clothes hanger. The only comfortable place to sit appeared to be the couch, but after waddling back to it, Mandilla reclined, looking for all the world like a beached blue whale.

I sat on the ladderback. Just as I was getting ready to talk, she spoke. "I'm ready," she said quietly.

"Pardon me?"

"Go ahead and prophesy," Mandilla said, waving a hand like an abbreviated flipper.

"I'm sorry. I don't know what you mean."

"The Book of Acts, chapter two, verse seventeen. *'In the last days, God says, I will pour out my spirit on all people. Your sons and daughters will prophesy.'* These are the last days, aren't they?"

"Of summer? I don't think so, dear. We still have the entire month of August."

"The last days of the *world.*" She regarded me with one eye closed. "You didn't come here to prophesy, did you?"

"No. I came to—"

Both eyes opened wide. "To ask my forgiveness? Hallelujah, praise the Lord! I've been waiting thirty years for this. Thank you, Jesus."

"Uh—for what am I being forgiven?"

"For your meanness, of course."

"What meanness?"

"In high school."

I could feel my lower jaw drop. "How was I mean?"

"You teased me all the time. You called me fat. You said I was ugly. You used to make squishing sounds when I walked by your desk. Everyone always laughed. Sometimes even the teachers."

"What?" I couldn't for the life of me remember ever having teased Mandilla Gindlesperger—only then it was Mandilla Beechy. I certainly never teased her about being fat. I was so rail-thin I would never have dreamed about making any comments pertaining to body shape. Stick, Bean Pole, Carpenter's Dream, those were the names kids called me, and they hurt. I would never have put anyone else through that sort of pain. And I most certainly never made squishing sounds to get the other kids to laugh. No one ever laughed with me in high school, it was always at me. And that included some teachers as well.

"The devil caused you to do shameful things, Magdalena, but with the Lord's help, I forgive you."

"Yes, but—"

"Say hallelujah, Magdalena."

"Hallelujah, but—"

"Say praise the Lord, Magdalena."

"Praise the Lord, but I never teased you," I wailed.

Mandilla smiled, one eye closed again. "Is the devil hardening your heart even now?"

"My heart's as soft as a three-minute egg," I cried, getting up from the ladderback chair. "And I didn't come to beg your forgiveness. I came to ask you a few questions about your doctor."

The smile disappeared as the eye opened. "There's

nothing in the Bible against doctors," she said. "Anyway it was Levi's idea that I go to one this time, seeing as how I began spotting early on. But Dr. Pierce, praise God, put me on some medication, and everything is fine. I wasn't supposed to work though—bed rest is what he ordered—but you can't lie in bed, what with twelve children."

"*Twelve* children," I said in wonder. Nothing appeared to be out of order in the living room. It was hard to imagine a dozen urchins clamoring about.

She took me wrong of course. "The Bible says, '*Be fruitful and multiply,*'" she said defensively. "Genesis, chapter one. Verse twenty-eight. Have you been fruitful, Magdalena?"

"I'm as barren as the Gobi Desert," I wailed, "but it isn't my fault!"

One eye closed again. "Perhaps if you submitted yourself to a man, Magdalena, your womb would blossom."

"I submitted!"

"Ah, yes, with the bigamist. But that was only last year. Already the vine had begun to wither. No, I'm talking about a submission of your will. If back when you were younger, Magdalena, you had not been so opinionated, if you had been meek and docile like God intended, you would have found your mate."

"*What?*"

"It's in the Bible. Colossians, chapter three, verse eighteen. '*Wives, submit to your husbands, as is fitting in the Lord.*'"

I had a lot to say about that, even things that were not commonly held to be true by my own denomination, but there is no point arguing theology with someone who belongs to a church with thirty-two words in its name. Besides, I was getting sidetracked.

"So you think Dr. Pierce is a good doctor?" I asked.

Both eyes were open wide. "Magdalena, is the desert blooming?"

"There's still a drought," I snapped. "I'm just asking on behalf of a friend of mine. Do you think Dr. Pierce is competent?"

"Of course."

"Do you know if he drinks?"

"Of course he doesn't! Well—not that I know of."

"Drugs?"

"Ach!" she said, displaying her origins.

"How do you feel about him taking off on vacation just when you're about to deliver? You *are* just about to deliver, aren't you?" Although, come to think of it, I'd seen on the cover of the *National Intruder* a photo of a colossal baby—forty pounds I think it weighed. Looked just like a miniature sumo wrestler. I do not buy the *National Intruder,* mind you, I merely glance at it when I'm in line at the grocery. I feel it is my duty to keep abreast of current events—even fictitious ones.

Mandilla looked stricken. For a minute I thought she was going into labor, and I was going to have to function as her midwife. Been there, done that, as the young folks say, and I'd rather have my nails ripped out and be force-fed mashed turnips than go through that again.

"I cannot tell a lie," Mandilla said, her voice quavering. "I quit seeing Dr. Pierce three months ago."

"Why?"

"Because, well, he didn't approve of what I wanted to do with my baby when he's born."

"And what is that?" I couldn't imagine what one did with a baby, besides raise it? Put it up for adoption? Sell it to the circus? Trade it to the gypsies?

"I'm giving it to the Lord," she said, and folded her flippers above her big blue stomach.

"What do you mean?"

"As you know, we already have twelve children— the same number as the disciples. We've decided to give the thirteenth one back to God."

"*How?* Shoot it up to Him in a rocket?"

"Don't be silly, Magdalena. Rockets don't really exist. Those are just little toys Hollywood uses to make us believe the devil's lies."

"I suppose you believe that man has never walked on the moon?"

"The Lord would never let him." She said it quietly and firmly, like a true and confident believer.

"Then just how do you plan to return this baby?"

"You take things too literally, Magdalena. Our son—and of course it will be a son—will be raised by a prophet."

"Let me get this straight, dear. You don't believe man has been on the moon, yet you're giving your baby away to Moonies?"

She shook her head. "He's not a Moony. He's the Prophet Elijah."

"You must believe in ghosts," I said, choosing my words kindly. "Elijah's been dead for thousands of years."

She closed both eyes. "I knew you wouldn't understand."

"Have you spoken about this with your pastor?" I asked gently. I knew Richard Nixon, pastor of the church with thirty-two words in its name He's not the brightest bulb in the clerical chandelier, but neither is he completely around the bend.

Mandilla's peepers popped open in alarm. "He may be my pastor, but not everything is his business."

"So then, he doesn't know. Well—"

"It's totally scriptural, Magdalena. Read your Bible. Hannah gave Samuel to the Lord."

I had no response to that, except for "that was then, and this is now," which seemed totally inadequate. There is no arguing with a fanatic. I would just have to take the time to call the Reverend Nixon and maybe Children's Services.

I stood. "How do your children feel about this?"

"They're honored that their little brother has been chosen to serve such a great prophet."

"Speaking of your children, where are they now? It's summer vacation. Shouldn't they be driving you crazy, screaming and yelling, and all the other bothersome things children do?" I'm ten years older than Susannah, and thus spent the bulk of my girlhood as an only child. Still, the way Mama told it, I was more trouble than a dozen husbands and as noisy as a gaggle of geese. A dozen children should have been exponentially louder and more burdensome, yet it was so still in the house I could hear the ticking of the plastic, sunflower-faced clock on the wall behind me.

The blue behemoth rose slowly from the bright plaid couch. "My oldest daughter Elizabeth Anne has them for the day. She and her husband have a nice place out in the country with a good fishing pond."

"You have a daughter old enough to be married and have her own place?"

Mandilla laughed. "Elizabeth Anne is twenty-seven-years old. You could have a daughter that old, Magdalena, if you'd been obedient and submitted your will to a man right out of high school."

"What?"

"It's too late for your shriveled womb to flower, of course, but it isn't too late for you to be a helpmeet to a man. In fact, there's a man who goes to my church— Warren Haywood—who is still unmarried. He's a little older than you, but at this late date you can't afford to be picky. You know that the Lord works in mysterious ways, don't you? Well, you might want to consider the possibility that the Almighty sent you here today so that I could fix you up with Warren."

I knew the man in question. His name should be Hay*seed,* not Haywood. He picks his teeth with the handle of a rattail comb, and despite his deep religious convictions, spits great frothing globs of tobacco juice wherever he goes. A barefoot, blindfolded person could track him just as easily as could a coon dog.

"In a pig's ear!" I wailed and fled the Gindlesperger house before the Almighty could play His divine practical joke and yoke me to the yokel Warren.

I have been criticized for being rigid with my meal schedule at the PennDutch, but so be it. The Good Lord intended us to eat breakfast at seven, lunch at noon, and supper at six, and although I can't find that passage in the Bible, I'm sure Mandilla Gindlesperger could. Come to think of it, there's probably a passage or two about table manners. I have no doubt the disciples chewed with their mouths closed, and if they put their elbows on the table, I'm sure the Lord gave them a good hard poke with his fork. He was here to set an example after all.

So you see, as a Christian it is my duty to insist on

punctuality and propriety. I insist that my guests be on time to all meals, and that they are properly dressed. No sleeveless dresses, no tank tops, no shorts. If it needs to be shaved, it must be covered at the table. Faces are the only exception.

Imagine my mortification, then, when I pulled into my driveway at quarter after six. Not only was I late, but there was no supper to serve. I put my pocketbook up to cover my face and sneaked into the kitchen through the back door. I hadn't the foggiest notion what I was going to make for supper. I can read and follow directions, but I lack the instinct to improvise, the mark of any really good cook, if you ask me. It is Freni's hand that rocks the ladle in this establishment. She plans all the meals, and although I do the bulk of the shopping, only Freni is allowed to put things away. She has her own system of organizing, one so bizarre and nonsensical that I can only conclude that in a past life Freni worked for the U.S. government. At any rate, I am forbidden to rummage through the cupboards, and consequently am at a total loss in my own kitchen.

The back door sticks, especially in humid summer weather, and it took a bit of shoving and grunting to get it open. When it did open it swung back all the way and sent me flying headlong into the middle of the room, only to be stopped by my massive kitchen table. It hit me mid-thigh and I toppled like a corn-stalk in a windstorm, landing facedown in something warm, moist, and, well, fairly tasty.

Fourteen

I looked up, licking my lips. Whatever it was, it wasn't half bad.

"Bubble and squeak," Edwina squeaked. I could tell them apart because Edwina still had her hair pulled back in a ponytail, her mole inexplicably much larger now.

I stared at the group seated at my kitchen table. They had plates of food in front of them and appeared to be about to eat. In addition to the twins, there was Vivian the leather-skinned vamp, her boy-toy Sandy, and the wholesome Redigers, both looking freshly scrubbed, their full Mennonite cheeks glowing with good health and godliness.

"What's going on?" I demanded.

Edwina twirled the tip of her tail with a short plump finger. "We knew you had a lot on your mind, so we all decided to pitch in and help out with dinner. The bubble and squeak is left over from lunch, but Daphne's made a nice curry, and Mr. and Mrs. Rediger brought a lovely cake back with them."

"Thank you," I said.

Vivian Mays waved a gold bangle in my face to get my attention. "Cooking has never been my forte. Besides, I'm paying you good money for that. This," she said, pointing to the repast in front of us, "is not up to par."

I smiled patiently. After all, the woman had pronounced forte correctly, not stressing the E, which would have made it quite a different word.

"Now I remember. I didn't get a chance to explain A.L.P.O. to you. You see, for a slightly higher rate you get the privilege of living like real Amish and preparing your own meals."

"Well, in that case."

"But we—" Gloria tried to butt in.

"You brought that lovely cake, dears."

The twins exchanged glances and giggled. I hastened to shut them up.

"Where's Dr. Barnes?" I asked.

The twins giggled again.

Gloria smiled. "He's in the dining room. We asked him to join us, but he refused."

Vivian nodded, her heavy necklace clanking like chimes in a stiff March wind. "He said eating in a kitchen is uncouth."

I wiped mashed potatoes off my face. "He's right. Especially when there's a perfectly good dining room going to waste. Did I tell you that table was built by my great-great-great-grandfather Jacob 'The Strong' Yoder? He made it from a tree that was growing on the very spot where the dining room sits today."

"Fascinating," Daphne said. "You Americans are so creative."

"Shall we move then?" I said.

"Let's!" Edwina clapped her pudgy palms. "This is going to be exciting."

"I'm glad to hear that. You English have such an appreciation for history—of course, yours is much longer than ours. Still, Jacob 'The Strong' was born in 1757. Or was it later? Yes, it had to have been much later. 1757 was the year another of my ancestors, Jacob Hochstetler, was taken captive by the Delaware Indians. He and two of his sons. Now that's a really interesting story. Would you prefer to hear it?"

Edwina flushed. "Actually, I meant it was going to be interesting dining with the professor."

"Oh?"

"He's so eccentric," Daphne said. "If you don't mind my saying so," she added.

"By all means, dear, call the kettle black."

"I beg your pardon?"

"It's just a silly expression," I said, hoping they didn't have the same one back in Manchester, England.

"He's weird," Sandy the sex slave had the nerve to opine. His head was tilted, and one of the pearl and platinum earrings was out of kilter.

Vivian Mays gave her new hubby a quick, disapproving look. I had the feeling their marriage was going to last no longer than last week's milk. *That*, at least, can be made into sour cream.

"None of us is perfect, dear," I said. "In fact, once in a moment of weakness I—"

The phone rang in the front lobby, saving me from an embarrassing confession.

"PennDutch Inn," I said gratefully. I was out of breath, having vaulted through the dining room, no doubt startling the absentminded professor.

"Did you find my little namesake?"

"Freni! How is Mose?" In the background I could hear someone paging a Dr. Killdeer.

"Ach, you would never know he was operated on. The man has the constipation of a horse."

"That's *constitution*, dear. And how are you doing?"

"Fine. Magdalena, did you find my baby?"

Her baby? To hear Freni, one would think *she* carried those babies around for nearly nine months. I swallowed a throat full of sarcasm.

"I haven't found any missing babies, dear."

"But you promised!"

"I said I would do my best."

"Your mama was a nervous woman, Magdalena. I'm not saying she didn't love you, but . . ."

"But what?"

"Ach, it isn't right to speak bad of the dead, Magdalena, but there is no other way to say it." She took a deep breath. "Your mama knew as much about babies as a hen knows about ducklings. It was me who took care of you, Magdalena. I am the one who fed you and wiped your skinny red bottom."

"Why I never!"

"Yah, you never once said thank you. Not that I can blame a child, but now, well . . ." Her voice trailed again.

"You can have my firstborn," I wailed.

Mercifully, Freni failed to remind me that I was as barren as the Gobi Desert, as fruitless as the Kalahari, as sterile as the Sahara. "You want to show your thanks, Magdalena?"

"Of course, dear." Thank the Good Lord she couldn't see my eyes, which were rolling like the wheels of a truck on the turnpike.

"Then find Little Freni!"

"I'm doing my best, Freni. In fact, I've been following a few leads."

"Yah?"

"Yah," I said, and then flushed with shame. "Freni, dear, do you know Rebecca Zook? The one who until just recently was working at Miller's Feed Store?"

"Ach, such a sad story."

"Oh?"

"There are rumors, Magdalena."

"What sort of rumors?"

Freni sighed, delighted to have my rapt attention. "She's in the family way."

"I know that, dear. It isn't a secret—*oh,* you mean she isn't married. Is that it?"

"Yah, but there is more."

"Do tell!" The ninth commandment forbids us to give false testimony against our neighbors. It does not forbid true testimony. Besides, Proverbs, chapter eighteen, verse eight says, *"The words of a gossip are like choice morsels, they go down to a man's inmost parts."*

Freni took a deep breath, nearly sucking my ear into the phone. "They say she bundled with an English man and—"

"Get out of town!"

"What? You want I should tell this story or not, Magdalena?"

"I want! 'Get out of town' is only an expression I learned from Susannah. Go on with your story, dear."

"Do you know what this bundling is, Magdalena?"

"Yes, but I want to hear more." Boy, did I! Supposedly, the custom originated some centuries ago in the cold, unheated farmhouses of Switzerland, but persists to this day among some Amish groups, especially here in Hernia, Pennsylvania. It is a controversial subject, even among the Amish themselves. I had heard references to bundling as long as I can remember, but had never had the nerve to ask Freni for details. Mama, a Mennonite born and bred, looked down her long Yoder (and not only by marriage) nose at the custom, calling it "sinful" and "an abomination." Of course Mama was also of the opinion that Mennonites should never engage in sex while standing, lest it lead to dancing.

At any rate, beyond the age of sixteen Amish teenagers are given an astonishing amount of leeway, known as *miteinander rumschpringe,* or literally, "running around together." This is the age when dating begins. If a relationship becomes serious, some Amish will permit the young people to cuddle, in *bed,* in a horizontal position. More often than not a rough board is placed between the couple to prevent any direct physical contact. In some Amish communities, however, the couple may actually embrace, but only from the waist up. One Amish church in the area insists that the young men remain fully clothed, but the young women may remove their dresses, as long as they remain in their petticoats!

Freni mumbled something that let me know she didn't approve of bundling altogether. No doubt this disapproval extends to Jonathan and Barbara's marital relations—or it may be *because* her son married a woman she couldn't stand (*i.e.,* any woman).

"But from what I hear, Magdalena, the Zooks practice this custom."

"With or without the board?"

"Ach!" She paused. "Without. And now they are paying the price."

"But with an *English* man?"

"Yah, a young boy who comes into the feed store now and then."

"You're saying the Zooks allowed their daughter to date an English boy?"

"Ach, so dense, Magdalena. Maybe they don't allow such a thing, but if they practice the bundling—well, you see what happens?"

In Freni's court the Zooks had been tried and convicted of parental neglect, or worse. It was time to steer the conversation away from the irresponsible parents and back to Rebecca.

"Is there any possibility of marriage?"

"Ach!" The sound of boulders crashing into my ear was a clue that Freni had dropped the phone on her end.

"Freni? Are you okay?"

"Yah," she panted, "but such nonsense you talk. Maybe the Zooks are not such good parents, and maybe Elizabeth is not such a good housekeeper—and her pie crusts are too dry—but they would never let Rebecca marry an English."

"They would shun her?"

"Yah, of course!"

Of course. Shunning is a major tenant of *Ordnung,* the Amish code of behavior. Members of the community are required to shun those individuals who have been excommunicated for grievous sins. These sins range from persistent playing of the radio (despite grave warnings) to adultery. The act of shunning is not a token slap on the wrist. One is forbidden to talk to, sleep with, and even eat with a shunned person. Fortunately, this need not be a permanent situation. If the sinner is truly repentant and promises to change his or her ways, they can be reunited to the community, both physically and spiritually. If the sinner is intransigent, the shunning could go on forever.

Spiritual insubordination can sometimes have disastrous consequences. Take the Troyers, for example, who live just down the road from me. He was excommunicated for pridefully installing rubber tires on his buggy. That was six months ago, and since then, by all accounts, Daniel and Lizzie Troyer have been living in separate parts of the house. Meanwhile Daniel refuses to repent for something which he does not view as a sin. In fact, I have seen him drive past my house in that very buggy, flaunting those comfy tires in broad daylight!

Unfortunately, but as might be expected, Daniel's parents, siblings, and numerous cousins think the bishop—who is a first cousin to Lizzie—has been too harsh. Lizzie's family, and reportedly herself included, support the bishop. There is speculation now that this particular congregation will split in half, and those in favor of rubber buggy tires will establish a new church. This will undoubtedly mean the end of Daniel and Lizzie's marriage. The Troyer situation might even be funny if it were not for the fact that Jonathan and Barbara are in favor of rubber tires, whereas Mose and Freni are dear friends of Lizzie's parents, and thus quite against this seductive worldly comfort. When rubber tires threaten to divide my loved ones, it stops being a laughing matter.

"Freni, dear," I said softly, "is there any chance that Rebecca Zook will repent?"

"Who knows? The Zooks are a hardheaded bunch. So why do you want to know about Rebecca?"

"I thought she might be able to use a new friend," I said deftly. That was true, only I didn't expect that new friend to be me.

"The Zooks want these rubber tires," Freni said tartly.

"Maybe I could talk them out of them."

Freni snorted. I knew what she was thinking. I'm a car-driving Mennonite, for crying out loud. I couldn't possibly talk an Amish person out of anything that was bad for them. To the contrary, I was likely to buy them a one-way express ticket to you know where.

"Are they the same Zooks who live next to the Kauffmans on Zweibacher Road?" I asked cagily.

"Ach! Those are the Bontragers! Rebecca Zook lives in that big white house on Hooley Lane. The one right beside that terrible curve. Dead Man's Curve," she added in a whisper.

Virtually every Amish family in the area lives in a big white house, but I knew now exactly which one she meant. Last winter two Hernia high school boys were drag racing down Hooley Lane, when the car in front plowed head-on into a horse and buggy. Five members of the Stutzman family were killed outright, three others were critically injured, including the driver of the lead car. As for the poor horse, no amount of whispering could save his hide.

"Terrible about that accident," I said, and clucked appropriately. "So when are you coming home, Freni? Do you need a ride?"

"Visiting hours are over at eight," she said. "That nice Mennonite couple will be picking me up."

"The Redigers? Aren't they being just a little too nice?" Believe me, I'd known Freni my entire life. There was no way I could be jealous of two leaf-watching upstarts from Indiana. Even if they were fellow Mennonites.

"Such good people, Magdalena. Always so calm and

soothing. You could take a page from their dictionary."

"That's *book*," I wailed. "And the Redigers use rubber tires!"

Freni hung up. She obviously didn't have a comeback for that.

I stood for a moment in the front by the lobby phone. I could hear peals of laughter emanating from the kitchen. A surreptitious peek into the dining room revealed the professor devouring a tome along with his meal. There was a scowl on his forehead. Clearly, neither party needed me.

They say that when the going gets tough, the tough get going. They may be right in this case. I got going— right out the front door and straight into the lap of temptation.

Fifteen

Bubble and Squeak*

✦

2 cups cold mashed potatoes
1 cup cold roast beef, shredded
1 cup cold steamed or boiled cabbage,
    chopped finely
1 medium onion, chopped finely
2 ounces sharp cheddar cheese
4 slices bacon
Salt and pepper to taste

Fry bacon until crisp, and remove from pan. Mix and shape remaining ingredients into four large patties. Fry for about five minutes on each side until hot through and golden brown. Garnish with crumbled bacon.

*This is a simple dish with as many variations as there have been men in my sister's life. For a heart-smart low-fat version use only the potatoes, cabbage, and onion. Fry in olive oil.

Sixteen

I have a new neighbor. The farm across from me, the one where my erstwhile Pooky Bear, the bigamist who took my precious flower and tore it asunder, used to live, this farm has been sold to an immigrant. Dr. Gabriel Rosen—a *medical* doctor in this case—doesn't hail from someplace overseas, but from New York City. The Big Apple, as he calls it. Urban refugee is what he calls himself.

Hernia has seen a lot of urban refugees lately. Our clean air, cheap prices, and uncongested streets are appealing to folks from Pittsburgh, Philadelphia, and in Gabriel's case, even much farther away. To be honest, we locals regard these newcomers with a mixture of awe and contempt. They buy our most expensive houses, or build enormous new ones, but then they wander about in blue jeans, or shorts that barely cover their fannies.

Although Dr. Rosen wears blue jeans, he is not like the rest. And he is not an urban refugee, no matter what he says. It was clear from the moment I met him that Gabe, as I now call him, was running *to* something, not *from* something. Gabe came west seeking solitude and a place to begin his new career, that of a writer. One has to admire a man who gave up a three-hundred-thousand-dollar salary at one of the nation's most prestigious heart clinics to write books. Either that, or mark him off as crazy.

Gabe is not crazy. He is, however, drop-dead gorgeous. Taller than I by at least two inches, he has warm brown eyes and a head of dark curly hair, so thick and beautiful it is all I can do not to reach out and run my hands through it. In fact, I once dreamed that I ran my toes through his locks.

We haven't exactly been dating, Gabe and I, but we do seem to find the slightest excuse to run across Hertzler Road and borrow this or that, or share some trivial bit of news. Last Sunday he showed up to borrow a cup of lima beans, just as I was sitting down to lunch. Lima beans! Cooked ones yet! Freni stoutly denies having told Gabe that lima beans were on my lunch menu, which they were. Since Freni never lies, well—go figure, as Susannah would say.

I rang the doorbell, and seeing myself reflected in the windowpane, quickly tucked a wisp of hair behind my ear. I wear my mouse-colored hair in a bun, and although I possess several equine features, I am not altogether unattractive.

The door flung open and Gabe stood there in a pair of tight jeans and pale yellow golf shirt. He was barefoot, and in the long summer dusk I could see that he had deeply tanned, slender feet with high arches.

"I came to borrow a cup of lima beans," I said. Actually, I came to sound Gabe out about joining the staff of Hernia Hospital. That, and to gaze once again upon that heavenly face.

Gabe has a brilliant smile. He is, after all, a man who can afford the finest dental work available.

"Will half a cup of frozen mashed potatoes do?"

"Frozen?"

"I'm afraid it's a TV dinner tonight. I really can cook, you know, but I got wrapped up in the climax scene."

"Excuse me?"

He laughed and ushered me inside. "The chase scene. The one in which my protagonist single-handedly fights, in an alley, a gang of five Pakistani drug smugglers who pose as New York cabbies."

"Ah, so it's a mystery!" Gabe has been as close-mouthed about his book as my faux-husband was about the missing years of his life.

"Yeah, it's a mystery, all right. I didn't want to talk about it before because—well, I guess because I'm kind of superstitious. But now that I have just the dénouement remaining, it seems safe."

I settled back in the offered chair, a black, buttery soft Italian leather monster that practically hugged me. Gabe sprawled across a matching sofa. So many cows were giving their lives for furniture these days.

"What's the title of your mystery?"

"Haven't decided. Did I tell you my protagonist was a seventy-eight-year-old Yiddish-speaking grand-mother from the Bronx?"

"No!"

"Well it is. So I was tentatively thinking of *The Hand that Rocks the Dreidel.*"

I raised an eyebrow.

"A dreidel is like a little top. It's a children's game that's played at Hanukkah."

"Why a mystery?" I said. And *why* didn't he direct me to sit on the couch as well. I wouldn't have minded a little sprawling in my direction.

"I wanted to jump into writing with both feet, and

mysteries are the most demanding form of fiction there is."

"How so?"

"Literary and mainstream writers can wander all over the board. They can digress until the cows come home—I love that expression now that I'm living in the country. Anyway, a mystery has to have a plot, and everything in the book must somehow advance that plot."

"Will it have proper punctuation?"

He looked surprised. "Of course."

"I only say that because I hate books that omit quotation marks. That mountain book left me cold."

"Yes, but that was a literary novel. Those authors can get away with anything, including murder."

"What about romance?"

"I'm all for romance," he said, and winked.

I blushed. I'm sure of that. My face engorged with so much blood that my feet floated off the floor, as light and dry as Freni's biscuits.

"Care for some wine?" he asked.

"I don't drink." I may have said it emphatically.

"Nothing?"

"Water, juice, milk, tea, coffee—oh, and cocoa. I really love cocoa."

"Is this a religious thing?"

I felt my face burn. My feet floated even higher. Gabriel and I had almost nothing in common, I knew that. Maybe that's what made him so exciting. With Aaron I'd picked a forbidden fruit, but unknowingly. There had been no excitement in that. With Gabriel came a whole new territory of possible sins. The prospect of avoiding them all—or not—made me giddy.

"Wine is an abomination," I said calmly. "It says so in the Bible."

"It also says that it gladdens the heart."

"Maybe in *your* Bible."

He smiled. "Maybe we shouldn't discuss religion. Not just yet. I've got some diet cola on hand. How about that? Or is that forbidden too?"

"Of course not."

"It wasn't on your list."

"And neither was rudeness, but you seem to have no problem dispensing that."

Brown eyes studied my face solemnly. "I'm sorry. I guess I presumed too much."

"Just what exactly does that mean?"

"Well, I thought a little good-natured banter was okay."

It was such a trivial thing, his little gibe, yet somehow it was now a pivotal point. Either I got over my defensiveness, or this relationship was going nowhere. Did I tell you that Gabriel Rosen had the longest, darkest eyelashes I had ever seen on a man?

"Banter away!" I cried.

He grinned. "Sorry again. And if I step over the line now and then, call me on it."

"Will do."

"So, what do you want to drink? I could make cocoa."

"It's July, dear. Do you have any grape juice?" Maybe I couldn't drink wine, but was it so wrong to pretend?

"Straight up or on the rocks?"

"I beg your pardon?"

"Without ice, or with."

"Oh, I get it. Without. I don't want to dilute it." I

gave him what I hoped was a mischievous wink. The last time I winked at a man he thought I had a cinder in my eye and offered assistance to remove it. You can be sure I told Deacon Graber to keep his mitts off me. He wasn't *that* cute.

"I'll bring you a double," he said. "Extra strong." Then either he winked back, or he had a smoldering log in his left eye.

While Gabe retired to the kitchen, I studied my surroundings. The previous owners, the Millers, had hired a heterosexual interior decorator from Pittsburgh. The result was dreadful. But the place looked pretty good now. If it wasn't for the pheromones that had been bombarding me like sleet in November, I would have been worried.

I noticed a row of silver-framed photographs on the mantel. From where I sat some of the pictures appeared to be of children. I knew that Gabe wasn't married—I will never make that mistake again—but he had been at one time. "*Long* divorced," he described it. And I knew about a nephew. But I wasn't sure about children. I may be a tad bossy, but I'm not nosy.

I struggled from the comfortable embrace of the leather armchair and strode to the fireplace. A young man with a bad complexion grimaced at me on the left. No doubt the college-aged nephew. To his right two little girls, one blond, one dark, smiled through a paucity of teeth.

"My nieces," Gabe said, reading my mind.

I wheeled. I hadn't heard him return, but he was standing there all right, a pair of long-stemmed goblets in his hands.

"Here." He handed me a goblet.

"Thanks." I took the drink.

Gabe read my mind again. "Mine's grape juice too."

"You didn't have to!" I am ashamed to say that I was simultaneously relieved and disappointed.

"Actually, it will do me some good. I stirred a little pectin in mine. It helps with carpal tunnel syndrome."

"You don't say." I'd heard this tunnel syndrome mentioned by a number of my guests over the years, but I must confess, I still didn't get it. How did carpooling through a tunnel hurt one's wrist? That's a bit self-indulgent if you ask me. What happened to Mama and Papa in the tunnel—squished to death amid milk and jogging shoes—now *that* was painful. All the grape juice and pectin in the world couldn't have fixed that.

"Please, sit." This time Gabriel motioned to the sofa. My heart pounded in my bony chest. I sat, but not before spilling a smidgen of the purple juice on Gabe's white carpet. Fortunately I was able to rub it down, deep into fibers, where it was basically out of sight. I prayed Gabe wouldn't find the stain.

Unfortunately Gabe chose to sit in the chair I'd vacated. He struck a seductive pose, crossing his leg ankle at knee, just as Aaron used to do. I tried not to peek below his calf.

"So, how's this batch of guests?" he asked.

Torn into three equal parts as I was, guilt, disappointment, and the need to reproduce, it was all I could do to stutter. "W-w-what?"

"You have any Nazis in this group?"

I sighed. Somehow we'd gotten derailed to small talk.

"No, no Nazis—that I know of. Just a pompous professor, one set of giggly English twins, and a wealthy vamp and her boy-toy. Oh, and the nicest Mennonite couple you ever laid eyes on. But enough about me. Tell me more about you."

Gabriel sipped grape from his goblet. "There isn't much to tell. Compared to you, I've lived a boring life."

"Nonsense, dear. I'm sure there's lots I'd like to hear. For instance, do you have any children?" *If I was going to stray far enough afield to snag a Jewish divorcé, he better not have any hidden commitments.*

Gabe grinned. "I assure you that those are my nieces. Besides, they happen to be all grown-up now."

"You sure? No little babies tucked away in some secret love nest?" I said it laughingly, and it was meant to be a joke.

"Babies?" he asked, looking puzzled.

"Babies!"

As if on cue a baby wailed loudly.

"What's *that*?"

Gabe laughed. "That's not a baby, that's—"

The baby wailed piteously again, the sound coming from upstairs.

I was on my feet faster than a freshly branded heifer. "Lying's a sin," I hissed. "In both our Bibles!"

"But I'm not lying!"

The infant howled miserably.

"Yeah? Well, explain that, buster!"

"That's easy. That's—"

I didn't stay long enough to hear another word. I charged out of there like a bull from a holding pen, and didn't stop until I'd snorted back to the Penn-Dutch Inn and into the privacy of my room.

*   *   *

I was still seeing red the next morning. It had been almost a waste of time lying in bed, sleeping as I did in fitful snatches. The still functioning phone in the lobby had rung several times during the evening, but I had steadfastly refused to answer it. I had no vacancies, and I certainly didn't need any more trouble.

About nine-thirty, as I was preparing for bed, there had been a timid knock at the door. It was Gloria Rediger dutifully informing me that Freni was home again, safe and sound, and Mose was recovering nicely. She'd even swung by Hernia Hospital, and seeing that Barbara and the two male babies were sleeping peacefully, Gloria somehow managed to coax Jonathan to go home as well. I thanked Gloria for her help, although frankly, and this is a terrible thing to say, I was beginning to resent her. Under normal circumstances it would have been me taking care of my loved ones. Instead, thanks to Freni's phantom namesake, I had a surfeit of stress.

Perhaps you will understand then why I was not amused to see that, despite my early hour of rising, the Moregold twins were already in the kitchen frying sausages and eggs. A tower of toast was already in evidence.

"Where's Freni?" I demanded.

The twins looked at each other and shrugged.

"Mrs. Hostetler," I snapped. "The stout, cranky Amish woman whose husband had his appendix removed."

"Ah, her," Edwina said as she spooned some grease over a sunny-side up. "Donald and Gloria ran her back into town. But don't worry, they've already had their breakfast."

"And he was really nice about it," Daphne said. "Considering I accidentally broke both of his."

"What?"

"The yolks on Donald's eggs," Daphne said. She hung her head in shame. "But Edwina's good at it, aren't you, sis?"

"Sunny-side up, or easy over," Edwina said gaily. "Just tell me your preference. Or if you like, I can make you a nice cheese omelet."

I grabbed a slice of toast and bolted. Clearly I was not needed in my own inn. Besides, too much cheer before ten has been known to cause nausea.

Seventeen

I took Dead Man's Curve at a crawl. On the right side of the road, just opposite the Zooks' driveway, was a simple wooden stake commemorating the grizzly accident. Carved into the wood were the Pennsylvania Dutch words for Gone to Glory. When I was a car length or two safely up the long drive I breathed a sigh of relief.

Ours is a hilly terrain, even mountainous by some folks' standards. There are many curves, although none as deadly as this, where one can find large mirrors positioned so as to give home owners a view of the road. For what it's worth, most of the area Amish refuse to use reflecting devices, thinking them too vain. Instead, they opt for playing Dutch roulette every time they enter a highway.

There was no doorbell on the Zook house—they didn't have electricity—so I rapped loudly with knuckles as large and hard as walnuts. The front door opened a crack.

"*Mir welles nüt,*" a gravelly voice said. We don't want it.

"I'm not a tourist," I blurted. "I'm Magdalena Yoder, owner of the PennDutch Inn."

The door all but closed.

"I'm an Amish-Mennonite, for crying out loud. All my ancestors were Amish. I even have Zooks in my family tree."

The door crept open an inch or two.

Encouraged, I opened my mouth. "I'm also a cousin of Freni Hostetler—"

The door closed altogether.

"But I support rubber wheels!" I wailed.

The door opened slowly, just wide enough for me to see a stout woman about Freni's age and size. I didn't have time to savor the irony.

"What is it?" the woman demanded in a thick accent.

"I—uh, I would like to speak with Rebecca."

"Why?" Tiny eyes regarded me warily behind bottle-thick glasses.

"Well, because—well, Freni's daughter-in-law, Barbara, had twins yesterday, but Freni is convinced there should have been triplets, only of course there weren't, and somehow I got pressed into playing detective and coming up with the missing triplet, which I'm not even sure exists, and the only lead I have is that Dr. Pierce, who was Barbara's doctor, and who, I believe, also was originally Rebecca's doctor, has suddenly decided to go off on vacation, and can't be reached, and of course I'd like to ask him a few questions, but can't, so I'm making it a point to talk to as many patients of his as I can, and who knows, maybe I'll come up with some clue as to where he is, in which case I can ask him directly how many babies Barbara Hostetler was really expecting." After I got rolling, I said it all in one breath.

"Ach, you are even crazier than Freni." The door started to close.

"*Grossmudder,* please."

I stared at the young woman now standing in the doorway behind her grandmother. Rebecca Zook. I remembered her now. I just hadn't remembered her name. But her face—surely it was the most beautiful face God ever created.

I've seen Liz's famed eyes of violet, but they pale in comparison to Rebecca Zook's. Throw in a flawless complexion, symmetrical features, and raven hair—a rarity among Amish—the woman is simply stunning. Unlike yours truly. Unfortunately, when the Good Lord made me He didn't break the mold, He just put a bridle on it and said "giddyap." But Rebecca, now there was a woman who could make heads turn in any city in the world, and not just at a racetrack either. It was no wonder an English boy found her attractive.

"Can I help you?" Rebecca asked. Without any apparent shoving, and despite her size, she'd managed to insinuate herself between her grandmother and the door.

"May I come in?"

Violet eyes scanned the sky behind me. "It is a pleasant morning. Perhaps we could talk outside?"

Frankly, this irritated me. I am not, as I've said before, nosy. And I know the Amish homes to be plain with functional furniture, and only unframed landscapes taken from calendars to decorate the walls. But the very fact that I was obviously not wanted made it immensely attractive.

"I'm chilly," I said.

"Just a minute." Rebecca disappeared, leaving *Grossmudder* to stare at me.

"Pretty girl," I said.

"Ach, we are all God's children. One no different than the other."

"Except some of us are mere Mennonites and unworthy of being invited in." It was a mean thing for me to say, but I mumbled it, so the old lady couldn't hear me anyway.

"What did you say?"

"I, uh, said—"

I smiled gratefully at Rebecca who had returned bearing an enormous woolen shawl, and who without further ado came outside and draped it around my bony shoulders. The shawl was incredibly heavy and smelled of horses, appropriate for me perhaps, but the truth be told, I wasn't really cold.

"We can sit in these rockers," Rebecca said, pointing to a constellation of chairs at the far end of an unpainted wooden porch. She led the way with remarkable grace, given her condition. I followed ponderously, dragging the heavy shawl.

"Now," she said, when we were seated, "what is this really about?"

I must have looked surprised.

"There was a reporter here yesterday," she said. "A man from Philadelphia, I think. He was writing a story on rebellious Amish youth."

"Oh, my."

"Yah, it is very embarrassing for me. For my family as well."

"I'm sure it is. But I assure you, I have nothing to do with this reporter. I just want some information on Dr. Pierce."

"He is a good doctor." Her voice rose slightly, suggesting a question.

"That's what I don't know. Do you mind if I ask you a few questions?"

She glanced down at her watermelon of a belly, hidden by a blue broadcloth dress and crisp black apron. I, of course, am not an expert at such things, but I couldn't image she had much longer to go.

"I do not wish to talk about it. It was a sin, yah, and I made my confession. I will confess again when the baby has come."

"Confess twice?" I squirmed, hoping the shawl would slip from my shoulders. The morning sun was hitting me full on and I was burning up.

Violet eyes locked on my faded blue peepers. "The first time was to the bishop and two elders. I cannot confess like this in front of the congregation. That I will do later."

"I see. Of course. Look, I don't want to ask you anything embarrassing or personal, I'm just curious why you went to Dr. Pierce in the first place. Don't Amish women use midwives?"

"Yah." She looked back at the mound in her lap. "It was Kevin's idea."

"Kevin?"

"My—uh, the baby's father."

"The boy from work?" I shrugged the shawl loose and it fell to the floor with a whoosh and a thump. It must have weighed ten pounds.

Rebecca looked at the wrap and then at me. Had she not been so encumbered, she might well have leaped up and retrieved the darn thing.

"I'm fine now," I said. "So, tell me about Kevin. Why did he want you to see a doctor in Bedford?"

"This is not your business, Miss Yoder, but I will

tell you anyway. Kevin is not of our faith—he is English. I am sure you know that."

"Yes, I do."

She sighed. "Perhaps the world knows. The man from Philadelphia? Where would he hear such a thing?"

"Who knows? Somebody tells somebody and they tell a cousin in Philadelphia? And since we're not at war at the moment, it's news. Amish are very 'in' right now."

She looked puzzled.

"What I mean, dear, is the English find you fascinating."

She nodded vigorously. "Yah, this is so. But why?"

"That's a good question. I wish I knew." Truer words were never spoken. If I knew the answer to that question, I would capitalize on it for all it was worth. The Good Lord doesn't mind if we make a dollar, just as long as we give Him His tithe.

"Ach, it can be so much trouble at times. But it is a cross we must bear."

I wisely censored my tongue. It would do no good, only cause anguish, to inform Rebecca that in her case, some of the world's attention was undoubtedly due to her extraordinary looks, and not the peculiarities of her religious convictions.

"So, dear, it was Kevin who picked Dr. Pierce?"

"Yah. You see, Miss Yoder, it is Kevin who will raise the child."

"What?" I nearly fell off my rocker.

"The bishop and the elders," she spoke slowly, "have said this is God's will."

"She told them?"

Never shock a pregnant Amish girl unless you're

prepared to deliver her baby. Frankly, I was shocked as well. Of course I don't believe God is a woman, any more than I believe He's a man (oops, that "He" word again). It's just that I get irritated when folks talk about God's will as if they have a special pipeline to the Almighty. I guess I wouldn't mind so much if the messages pertained only to them, and didn't concern the affairs of others. Perhaps I wouldn't be so bitter if Reverend Lantz hadn't managed to persuade Mama that God didn't want me attending college at the University of Pittsburgh, where I might have pursued a degree in clinical psychology. Instead, the Good Lord communicated *through* Reverend Lantz that I would be much better off enrolling in Bedford Community College. I hope someday I'll find a use for my associate's degree in English up in heaven, because I have yet to find one for it here.

Fortunately Rebecca didn't go into labor, but she staggered to her feet. "I think you should leave now, Miss Yoder."

"I'm sorry!" I wailed.

"You have blasphemed."

"Yes, but I'm repenting. Please let me stay."

Violet eyes looked past me. "I cannot. I am in enough trouble as it is."

"Trouble? What trouble?"

"Shhh. *Grossmudder.*"

A second later I heard the front door close.

It was still the shank of the morning, and one slice of toast does not a breakfast make. Lacking any better leads, I had decided to drive the twelve miles into Bedford and poke around in the vicinity of Dr. Pierce's office, maybe even his home. Just outside of

Bedford, where Highway 96 hits the turnpike, sits the Sausage Barn. It's a new establishment, a backlash against the low-fat trend of the nineties. The Mennonite owners of the Sausage Barn subscribe to that time-honored Anabaptist tradition that fat is where it's at. Everything at the Sausage Barn comes swimming in grease of some kind, but the management makes up, in part, for this by banning smoking altogether. Here at the Sausage Barn nonsmokers get to eat their grease in peace.

Please understand, I am not espousing high cholesterol or advocating heart attacks. I am merely stating a fact: fat tastes good. Animal fat tastes the best. What can compare to a greasy strip of bacon, fried crisp on the ends, but with just a little play in the middle? Didn't the Good Lord forbid His Chosen People to eat pork, so that the rest of us could have more? Frankly, as a good Christian I consider it my religious duty to eat as much bacon as possible, thereby sparing Jews and Muslims temptation.

Freni cooks lavish, lard-laden breakfasts, but I still find regular excuses to visit the Sausage Barn. Breakfast is my favorite meal, and the Sausage Barn serves nothing but breakfast, twenty-four hours a day. I parked in what has become my usual spot, and was shown to my regular booth by Wanda, owner, receptionist, and sometimes server.

"Just one?" she asked. She asks that every time, although I invariably come in alone.

I forced a smile. "Yes. And I'd like my usual booth if it's available."

"You know," she said as we wound through a labyrinth of wooden stalls, most of them filled with diners, "you might get yourself a man if you put a little meat on those bones."

"I'm trying!" I wailed. "I mean, I'm trying to fill out a little. I've already got a man."

"Oh?"

I thought about Gabe the babe, who probably wouldn't be caught dead eating here, and besides he already had a babe of his own. At least a baby.

"Well, it's nothing serious. But I am seeing someone."

Wanda handed me a well-smeared plastic-coated menu. "You always ask to sit back here in the corner by the kitchen. Why is that? These are the last booths to fill, and nobody can see you back here. You're not going to catch a man that way."

"I'm not *trying* to catch a man! Besides, I like it back here because I can see the orders come up. Frankly, dear, Agnes is a little slow and needs prompting now and then. If I want cold eggs, I can get them at home."

"Agnes had polio when she was a kid. And she's mentally challenged. We at Sausage Barn do our best to be inclusive."

I slapped both cheeks—gently, of course—with my right hand. Someday, when ducks fly backward, I'll learn to curb my tongue.

Wanda pulled a well-chewed pencil out of a beehive that sat squarely atop her round little head. I'm not claiming that Wanda invented this hairstyle, but I know for a fact she's been wearing her hair that way ever since we were in tenth grade together. And I don't mean this to be unkind, but I don't think Wanda's washed that do in all these years.

"Agnes's legs are bothering her a bit this morning,

so I'll be covering some of her tables. What will it be? Your usual?"

"I don't come here all *that* often," I said defensively. "And I certainly don't order the same thing every time."

Wanda scribbled on her pad. It was a wonder a pencil that greasy could still write.

"Two eggs, poached well. Bacon, not too crisp. Pancakes, golden brown, but not too dry in the middle. Real maple syrup—none of those fancy fruit toppings. Large O.J. Decaf coffee with lots of half and half."

"You forgot the butter," I wailed. "I can't eat pancakes without butter."

Wanda pointed to a bowl already on the table. It was spilling over with individual pats.

"Leave it to me, hon. I know you like the back of my hand. You just leave everything to me. I'll get you a man."

"But I don't want a man!"

The cowbells attached to the front door clanked and Agnes bustled off to seat more guests. She was back before I could finish checking my tableware for water stains. In her tow was the arrogant and antisocial Dr. Barnes.

"This man says he'd like to meet some authentic Mennonites and Amish. You're an authentic Mennonite, aren't you, Magdalena?"

I sighed. "Good morning, Dr. Barnes."

"Good morning, Proprietress."

Wanda beamed. Her broad smile used so many muscles that the mound of hair teetered precariously. I leaned toward the window, away from the threatening do. It was a tense moment, I'll have you know. Should that beehive fall and unravel, it might well release a plague of disastrous proportions. Who knows to what extent vermin might have mutated in that thing over the past thirty years. I briefly considered the possibility that Wanda was part of a communist plot. The demolition of the Berlin Wall, the apparent unraveling of the Soviet Union, these might all be clever ploys to get this country off guard. Then one fine summer day Wanda Hemphopple of Hernia, Pennsylvania, pulls a simple hairpin out of her towering do, and the world's largest democracy is obliterated.

"So, you two already know each other?"

"Yes, this man's a guest at my inn. But why he can't be content to take his breakfast there is beyond me."

Professor Barnes had the temerity to slide into the booth and sit opposite me. "Perhaps if your establishment lived up to its claims, I would. Your brochure advertised an authentic Amish cook. So far it's been potluck, or eat the slop those English women serve."

"Well, I never!"

"That's right. You haven't been there to share in their dreadful meals." He waved away the proffered menu and looked accusingly at me. "I was here last night, also."

"In that case, would you like to order?"

Professor Barnes nodded. "Two eggs, please, poached well. Bacon. But not too crisp, mind you. I don't like it when it shatters. Hmm, and instead of toast, I'll have pancakes. And real maple syrup."

Wanda winked and the do wobbled. Annihilation was imminent.

"Professor, what would you like to drink?"

"A large orange juice and some decaffeinated coffee. Oh, and bring lots of half and half."

Wanda beamed again, this time so broadly that even the professor edged toward the window. "I can see that you two were meant for each other," she said, "so I'll leave you little lovebirds alone."

"Don't leave me!" I wailed to her rapidly retreating back.

The professor fixed his rheumy eyes on me. "I will be expecting a partial refund, of course."

"What?"

"Assuming my linens are changed today, and I get fresh towels. Otherwise I expect a full refund."

"You're off your rocker," I said, not unkindly.

"And about those pillows. Surely you can come up with something softer. Like maybe some rocks."

"Try your head, dear," I mumbled.

"While you're at it, Miss Yoder, I expect you to speak to the lad in Room Six."

My eyes widened. "Jacko?"

"I don't know his name. But at the rates you charge—well, a good night's sleep is not too much to ask. That jumping and hollering kept me up until the wee hours."

"He brought the chimp this time?" I've never asked the man just what it is he does with all those animals. But for the record, I much prefer the llama to the chimp.

Massive eyebrows met briefly, like two land crabs greeting each other at low tide. "If we're to use that rocker imagery, Miss Yoder, I'm afraid your rocker has gone off the porch entirely."

"How dare you insult me like that!"

"How dare you try and pass that horrible little town of Hernia off as the Pennsylvania Dutch capital of the country?"

"But it is!" That, of course, depends on how you define "is." And who said we have nothing for which to thank Kenneth Starr?

"Pshaw!" The pompous professor actually said that. I wouldn't lie on a stomach that was empty, save for one piece of toast.

"Well, we don't put the same commercial spin on our heritage here that they do in Lancaster County. But we have lots of Amish and Mennonites just the same."

"Are you even a real Mennonite?"

"Of course. Born and bred. Although technically, I've never actually been bred—"

"Miss Yoder!" he said, his voice sharp with impatience.

"That's Proprietress, dear. Remember?"

He stood. "That does it. You are simply impossible. I shall be finding new lodgings for tonight."

"Lodgings? Beavers live in lodges for Pete's sake. And Elks—the partying kind—hang out in lodges. The PennDutch is *not* a lodge, I'll have you know. And for the record, far finer folks than you have laid their heads on my pillows and slept just fine."

Dr. Barnes must not have been all that hungry, because he stalked off.

Although I was ravenous, I chased after him. I have been known to apologize, if it will bring a paying guest back. At any rate, I certainly did not intend to pay for his breakfast.

Alas, I hadn't gotten more than ten feet when I tripped, and fell right into the lap of trouble.

Eighteen

"**S**usannah!" I struggled to my feet. "What on earth are *you* doing here?"

"Watching you put the moves on that old dude, Mags. Really, sis, you could do better than that."

How could I not have seen my sister, sitting just two booths back, swaddled as she was in hot pink drapes? Love may be blind, not as blind as hunger.

"Look who's talking?" I wailed. "Besides, I wasn't putting the moves on Professor Barnes. I've already got a man, remember?"

"Who?"

"Susannah! You know darn well who."

"Oh, you mean that hunk who bought Aaron's old house? Did he finally ask you out?"

"No, he didn't ask me *out*. There's no need. He lives right across the road from me."

"So?"

"So, we're both mature adults, for crying out loud. We don't go on dates. We just get to know each other."

Susannah clapped her hands and squealed with glee. At least seven diners put down their forks to watch.

"Did you *do* it, Mags?"

"I beg your pardon?"

"The mattress mambo. The horizontal tango. The waltz of lust. Did you do it with Dr. Rosen?"

"Susannah!" I find it hard to believe that Susannah and I are related. Had I not been ten at the time she was born, and seen Mama just prior to, and soon after, the birth, I would have believed her story that Susannah was found under a cabbage. Due to a preponderance of evidence, I can only conclude that Mama was not the Goody Two-shoes she claimed to be, and that Susannah is the fruit of some English man's loins and, in some quirk of nature, my little sister received all her genetic material from her father, and none from our mother. Not a single drop of Amish or Mennonite blood flows through her veins, that's for sure. It seems probable that Susannah's papa was a Presbyterian—given her attraction to that faith—and quite possibly he was a fabric salesman. And since Mama would never have cheated on Papa while in her right mind, I must conclude that Susannah's father managed to intoxicate our mother. Of course, staunch Christian that she was, Mama would never have allowed alcohol to pass her lips. Therefore, it had to be something less overtly evil than booze, but just as discombobulating to the senses—like maybe marijuana brownies (not that I would know from experience, mind you). *So,* if you ever hear of a polyester-peddling, predestination-professing pothead, one who claims to have sowed his wild oats in Hernia in the early 1960s, let me know. I'd like to have a DNA test run on him.

My baby sister had already been served her food. She reached into a cloth-covered basket and withdrew a biscuit.

"You know, Mags, you should really get over this

hang-up you have about sex. It's a natural function. Just like eating."

"There are plenty of natural functions one doesn't discuss," I said. I reached for her bread basket. "May I?"

"What's mine is yours, sis."

I reached into the warm basket, taking care not to lift the cloth more than was absolutely necessary. A cold biscuit makes a good hockey puck, but that's it.

"What the—*ouch*!"

"Sssh, Mags! You don't want us thrown out, do you?"

"But the rat's in there!"

"He's not a rat, Mags, he's a dog. Besides, it's nice and warm in there."

"What's wrong with your bra? Or your purse?" In Susannah, the boundaries of what is normal reach new limits.

She broke her biscuit in half, the wrong way, and sighed. "He's been gaining weight, Mags. It's been getting a little uncomfortable for me. And I left my purse at home this morning."

I lifted the cloth napkin slowly. Beady black eyes blinked.

"Dog. Biscuits. Hmmm. I'm glad you didn't order French toast. I'm not sure this ticker could have taken it. By the way, dear, what are you doing here, and without a purse? You don't have a car, so how did you get here? And how do you expect to pay for breakfast?"

Susannah rolled her eyes. "You are such a worrier, Mags. I just came. I hitched a ride. And not having my purse with me is not such a big deal. I'm sure someone will pay for my breakfast. Things always work out if you let them."

I covered the basket again. For the record, I did not take a biscuit.

"You mean, don't you, if you let other people take care of you?"

"Oh, Mags, you always look on the negative side. Let yourself go and live a little."

That galled me. Susannah can afford to let go because she has me—and to some extent, Melvin— around for damage control. It just isn't fair that some of us have to toil, our considerable noses to the grindstone, so that others of us can party.

"You're thirty-five years old, dear. It's time you got a job."

"I had a job, remember? I got fired."

I remembered. Somehow Susannah got a job naming paint chips for a short-lived Bedford company, Crazy Paints. She even named an entire wheels of chips after me. *Magdalena Mania.* But the public wasn't ready for such outré nomenclature. Wrinkle White, Bowel Brown, Toenail Tan, these were not something folks wanted to use in decorating their homes.

"Get another job, dear."

Susannah gobbled what remained of her doggy biscuit and reached for another. Shnookums snarled, and Susannah wisely backed off. That minuscule mutt is not above mangling his mistress. In a minuscule, but nonetheless painful way, of course.

"I'll think about it. Now you tell *me.* What are you doing here? And with that man? You still haven't said."

"That man was Wanda's idea of matchmaking. It

just so happens that he is—or was—a guest at the inn. Our being here at the same time was totally coincidental. I'm on my way into Bedford to do an errand for Freni, and neglected to eat breakfast."

"Can I hitch a ride?"

"To where?" I couldn't imagine sleuthing with a slovenly, slutty, and slothful sister in tow. It would cramp my style.

"I don't care where. I'm not doing anything special today. And it's so boring at home."

"It wouldn't be if you had children—" I pinched myself hard. Yes, I longed to hear the pitter-patter of little nieces and nephews, but was willing to wait until my sister came to her senses, divorced Melvin, and married someone human.

Susannah shrugged. "Maybe you're right. Maybe I should just go home. Melvin said he was going to try and find time to swing around to the house on his break, and at lunch. That's two tries for children right there."

I sighed. "Okay, you can come along. But you have to keep your mouth shut about what you see or hear today. You can't breathe a word of this to anyone. Especially *Melvin*. Do you promise?"

"Ooh, Mags, what are you up to?"

"Promise?"

"I promise."

"I'm looking for clues about Freni's lost grandbaby."

"The one that doesn't exist."

"That's the one, only—well, I know this is going to sound weird, but I have this strange feeling he—make that she—really exists."

"Wow, Mags, you turning psychic?"

I shuddered. We Mennonites eschew anything to do with the occult, fortune-telling, or the like. We believe firmly that God, and only God, is the author of our fates. We also believe in free will. When I've figured out that paradox, I'll let you know.

"I am most certainly *not* turning psychic. But I have a hunch." Hunches are, incidentally, theologically okay. And just so you know, one hunch from a woman is worth two facts from a man.

"Wow! This is so cool! A little niece!"

"Cousin," I reminded her patiently. "But like I said, it's a hunch, and I'm a long way from proving it. In fact, I don't even know where to begin."

"Let me help!" I don't recall ever seeing Susannah so animated.

"I was hoping you'd say that."

"Really?"

"Really. Tell me everything you know about Nurse Hemingway."

"My friend Hemmy?"

"That's the one."

Before my sister could as much as open her mouth, Wanda delivered our meals. Susannah got the omelet and sausages she ordered. I got *two* sets of bacon and poached eggs.

I raised my eyebrows.

"You're paying for both," Wanda said archly. "You may as well eat 'em."

"I meant, where's my pancakes, dear?"

Wanda pointed to the short stack at my elbow.

"That's only one, dear. I get two, remember?"

Wanda stomped off in a snit. I turned to Susannah.

"So, dear, what do you know about this Hemmy person?"

"Wait just one minute, Mags. What does my friend have to do with some doctor's mistake?"

"Probably nothing. It's just that Nurse Hemingway said she heard that Dr. Pierce—Barbara's original OB-GYN—was a heavy drinker. Another source of mine says he wasn't. Do you think Nurse Hemingway could be lying?"

"Hey, Mags, I resent that. Just because I stretch the truth sometimes doesn't mean my friends do."

She had a point. "All right, dear, I'm sorry. So, what can you tell me about her? I hear she's from Pittsburgh. She ever talk about that?"

Susannah yawned. "Get real, Mags. We don't talk a whole lot. We just have fun."

"Fun?"

"Sometimes after she gets off work, if Melvin's not home, we go out for a drink. Well, several drinks, really. But only beer," she added quickly.

"That's fun?" Maybe it was fun to hear Mama turning over in her grave. I couldn't imagine it was fun to actually drink. Once in college I yielded to temptation and took a sip of beer. I did *not* swallow it, mind you. I merely tasted it. It reminded me of the girls' locker room in high school.

"Oh, Mags, you need to lighten up. Live a little!"

"I do," I said stiffly. "So, you don't really know Nurse Hemingway all that well, do you?"

"Yeah, I know her. I know she likes guys with tiny butts." Susannah giggled.

"That's it? You drink the devil's tea together, and that's all you've learned?"

"Hey, I don't pry. Not like some people."

I let that roll off, like sewage from a drunk's back. "Have you ever been to her house?"

"Nah. She claims she's even messier than me."

"Than *I*."

"Nah, you're pretty neat."

"I meant—never mind. Let's eat."

Of course I said a blessing before we dug in, and of course Susannah rolled her eyes and slid low in her seat. Heaven forbid she should be caught thanking the Good Lord for the food He had provided. I quite wisely withheld any criticism and we dug in, eating in silence, except for a few grunts I directed toward Wanda when she returned with my second short stack. Wanda grunted back. The Sausage Barn seemed to be thriving, despite the owner's lack of manners and poor hygiene.

To keep Wanda on her toes, and as a favor to her future customers, I didn't leave a tip.

I decided there wasn't much point going to Dr. Pierce's office. It would be locked, and I wasn't about to break and enter. Not in broad daylight.

Instead I would swing by Dr. Pierce's house in Bedford, and just casually drop in. Yes, he was supposed to be away on vacation, but that didn't mean anything. There have been times when I've officially been away from the PennDutch, but still been in residence, if you know what I mean. That month of my pseudo-marriage to the bigamist Aaron—well, that really isn't your business, is it?

At any rate, I hadn't driven more than a mile down the pike toward Bedford when Susannah let out a shriek worthy of any Yoder, living or dead. No doubt it woke the dead, even several counties over. Come Judgment Day my baby sister would make an excellent addition to my rousting team. It was a wonder we didn't wreck.

"What is it?" I gasped with my first available breath. I had managed to get us to the side of the road by then, and I was shaking like the paint-mixer at Home Depot.

"My baby," Susannah screamed. "I forgot my baby!"

I could feel the blood draining from my equine face. "Shnookums?" I asked weakly.

"He's still in the biscuit basket! Oh, Mags, we have to save him!"

I made an illegal U-turn, cutting across a woods-filled median, and pressed the pedal to the metal. Fortunately it was a slow traffic day, and besides, there were no troopers about. If I had been caught, how-ever, I would have deserved a taxpayer's vacation in the hoosegow.

"Faster!" Susannah cried.

"I'm going as fast I can, dear." There was no need to urge me on. If Wanda caught the hound from Hades in her restaurant, much less wallowing about in a biscuit basket, I would no doubt be banned for-ever from the Sausage Barn. Not leaving a tip could be interpreted as an oversight, but a pile of poop from a pathetic pooch is at best problematic.

"Save the life of my child," cried the desperate mother.

I did my best. My new red BMW has a lot of horses under the hood, and I got the entire herd galloping at full speed. I wouldn't say that we broke any land records, but it is a fact that once we stopped it took a moment for my breath to catch up with us. I'm pretty sure our shadows took a while as well, although I didn't stick around long enough to see.

Susannah sailed into the Sausage Barn, a swirl of hot pink fabric, and swept right past Wanda, who was again playing hostess. I raced after her.

"Where do you think you're going?" Wanda yelled.

"We forget something," I puffed.

"You're damn right. You forgot my tip."

I was so worried about the bitty beast it barely registered that Wanda had used a naughty word.

"Shnookums!" Susannah cried, suddenly spotting the biscuit basket still on the table. She ran toward the booth, her arms outstretched, her wardrobe streaming behind her.

Wanda caught up with me, grabbing my arm. "What is your crazy sister up to now?"

I glared at Wanda Hemphopple. "She isn't crazy, she's emotionally challenged."

"Nonsense. Your sister is as nutty as my world-famous peanut brittle."

"*Your* peanut brittle? Your stole that recipe from Florence Root!" I have forgotten to mention that although the Sausage Barn serves only breakfast, they have a mouth-watering selection of homemade candies up by the register.

"I didn't steal that recipe," Wanda hissed. "I merely guessed at the ingredients."

Out of the corner of my eye I could see Susannah reaching for the basket on the still-cluttered table. We were almost out of the woods. If I could stall Wanda for just a few seconds longer, we could beat a hasty retreat and Wanda would be none the wiser.

"What kind of a woman checks for tips, but doesn't clear the table?"

"A busy woman."

"Ah, but you swore," I said, grabbing at straws.

Wanda recoiled, her beehive vibrating fast enough to create a breeze. "I did not!"

"You most certainly did. You said the D word. And you a Mennonite!"

"For your information, Magdalena, I am not a Mennonite. I'm a Baptist, and we're allowed to swear. We're even allowed to dance. We just can't go to Disney World."

"Well, you shouldn't swear in front of customers—" I stopped, my heart had left its perch in my bony chest, and was flailing about in my stomach among the remains of four poached eggs, six strips of bacon, and six pancakes.

My baby sister was headed straight for us, her arms extended like a child wanting to be picked up. Her face was ashen, and she was moaning something. I folded her protectively into my arms.

"What did you say?" I rasped.

Nineteen

"**H**e's gone," Susannah moaned. "My baby's gone."

"But the basket's still there!"

"What's this all about?" Wanda Hemphopple demanded, hands on hips.

"It's a family matter," I said.

Wanda scratched her head. The towering do wobbled precariously.

"Your sister doesn't even have a baby, so she couldn't have lost it. I'm not about to be held responsible for a child who doesn't exist."

"But he—"

I clamped a hand over Susannah's mouth. "She calls her purse 'baby.'" Okay, okay. But it wasn't a total lie, since she does call Shnookums "baby," and he's often *in* her purse.

Wanda shook her head. I flinched.

"I didn't see a purse, Magdalena. And no one's turned one in."

"Well, maybe one of Susannah's friends saw it and is keeping it safe for her. Mind if we circulate a bit?"

"I most certainly do!"

Fortunately a family of five walked in the door. They just weren't any family, either, but the Augsbergers, a clan known hereabouts for eating prodigious amounts of food. Along with the cowbells on the door, Wanda could no doubt hear the cash register ring. She waltzed over to the group, and immediately began fawning. You would have thought the Queen of England herself had arrived.

Susannah and I wasted no time. We split up. The Sausage Barn is laid out along two main aisles. Susannah took the aisle where we'd been sitting; I took the far aisle.

Granted, it looks suspicious to peer under tables around which folks are dining, but a gal's got to do what a gal's got to do. Since no one in the restaurant was screaming, it was safe to assume that the mini-monster was holed up under a table, chowing down on crumbs. And yes, I got dirty looks, and a few unpleasant comments, but I'm forty-five years old, for Pete's sake, and an orphan. I can do what I want.

"Hellooo," a young man cooed, "if I would have known this was going to happen, I would have worn shorts. *Baggy* shorts."

I picked up a fork that had fallen, gave him a poke, and moved on.

"Mama, there's a witch under the table," a little girl whined.

Her shoelaces were untied, so I tied them, *together,* before beating a hasty retreat.

"My, my, how the mighty have fallen." I recognized the nasal voice of Lodema Schrock, my pastor's wife. "Guess who's scavenging with the dogs, just like Lazarus."

I bumped my head on the underside of the table. "Dogs? Did you see a dog?"

"That's from the Bible, Magdalena. If you didn't skip church so often, you'd know that."

I'd only missed church once in the last six months, and that's because I had the flu. A pastor's wife should be more careful about making accusations. One of Lodema's shoes had slipped off, and to teach her a lesson, I tucked a wad of scrambled egg in the toe.

The diner at the next table was even more hostile than Lodema. "Come out from there, right now," he growled, "or I'll have you arrested for indecent exposure."

Me? A pair of Lilliputian legs dangled in front of me. The trousers above the legs were clearly open, no doubt to accommodate an expanding belly.

I crawled out. "Look, buster, you—you're Dr. Bauer!"

"Indeed I am. Do you often go about on all fours, Mrs. Hostetler?"

I glared at the gnome, but small as he was, I found him intimidating. I stared at his pancakes instead. Unlike Dr. Barnes and myself, Dr. Bauer preferred those perfume-sweet artificial syrups. His half-eaten pancakes were practically floating.

"I am *not* Mrs. Hostetler, I'm Miss Yoder. And that stuff will rot your teeth, you know."

"Is this your expert opinion?"

"Frankly, yes. I did in a perfectly good set of baby teeth that way. And from what I recall, you have the smallest teeth—"

"Mags!" Susannah grabbed my arm, and with surprising strength pulled me away from the dinky doc and his soggy stack.

"What is it, dear? Did you find him?"

Susannah nodded, but I saw terror in her eyes, not joy. "Look over there."

"Where?"

"There, by the register. Look at Wanda."

I looked. Wanda Hemphopple was taking advantage of a lull to sort some receipts that had been speared on a miniature pitchfork. There, immediately above the crest of Wanda's beehive, was the wicked little face of Shnookums Stoltzfus. His beady black eyes glistened like caramelized raisins, his pointed ears stuck straight up. Frankly, he looked smug and content.

"Oh, my gosh!" I staggered and had to steady myself on the nearest table.

"And now you dare take the Lord's name in vain!" Lodema said. She sounded positively jubilant.

"I most certainly did not!" For some reason Lodema's attitude gave me fortitude. It was now I who pulled Susannah along with surprising strength.

"Oh, Mags, what are we going to do?" she wailed.

"Don't worry, dear, I'll think of something. I know—we'll get as close as we can to the old battle-ax. Then I'll do something to get her to look down, and then you snatch Shnookums. When you've got him, stick him in your bra and run like the dickens."

Two tables cleared just then and we had to wait while the Gingriches and Roches paid for their meals. Esther Gingrich has eyes like a hawk, but mercifully, even she didn't spot the mutt in the mane.

When the coast was clear Susannah and I sidled up to the register. I held out a five-dollar bill.

"Wanda, dear, here's the tip I forgot."

Wanda looked startled. I have noticed that kindness has that effect on folks, at least coming from me.

"Well, thanks."

But before she could grab the tip from my hand, I dropped it. The bill drifted toward the floor like an autumn leaf. For a second Wanda stared at the money, and then she scrabbled after it, like a kid after candy when a piñata has been broken. The beehive sank beneath the level of the counter.

"Quick!" I yelled.

Susannah needed no urging. She is only an inch shorter than me, and it was a fairly easy thing for her to lean over the counter and snatch the incorrigible cur from its den of dander. She shoved the ungrateful thing into the recesses of her swaddled bosom and slipped outside. I was hard on her heels.

Susannah and I laughed all the way into Bedford. We were still laughing when we pulled up to Dr. Igna-cious Pierce's house. We stopped laughing and stared. Not only was the place immense, it was a bizarre com-bination of Tudor and medieval castle. Turrets com-peted with massive beams for attention, while half the roof was covered in slate, the other in wooden shin-gles. It was the most grotesque residence I had ever seen.

"Ooh, Mags, I love it!"

"Gag me with a spoon," I said. I may not be of this world, but I have picked up some of its hipper phrases.

At any rate, it hadn't been hard to find the OB-GYN's residence, as it was listed in the white pages. Since there are no sidewalks in this ritzy part of town, we parked boldly in the driveway. Our plan was to pretend that we "belonged." Given Susannah's uncon-ventional attire, however, and my rather conservative frock, we looked more like representatives of two competing religions out to save the doctor's soul.

There were no other cars in the driveway, and the four-car garage lacked windows, so we merrily marched up to the door and rang the bell. No one answered right away, but we waited patiently.

"Man, I could live in a place like this," Susannah said with a sigh.

"Indeed, you could. All it takes is determination."

"I don't even think so."

"But it's true. *If* you really wanted a place like this, you could have one."

"How? Just by wishing?"

"No, of course not. You could"—I chose my words carefully—"get a job. Then you and Melvin could put yourselves on a strict budget, and invest part of your earnings. It might take a while, and it might not be very much fun, but eventually you'd have a nice nest egg."

Susannah rolled her eyes. "Man, you can be a downer sometimes, Mags, you know that? I was just daydreaming, and then you go and get all serious on me."

"Well, *excuse* me!" I pumped the bell, irritated now that our camaraderie had been so fleeting. When after another minute or two no one had answered, I tried the knob. I tried it out of exasperation, not because I actually expected the door to open. But it did.

"Holy Moly!" Susannah cried.

We stared into a foyer that was every bit as big as mine back at the inn. This one had a parquet floor that was partially covered by a thick, fancy-shmancy rug that might well have been genuine wool. A spiral crystal chandelier hung from an unnaturally high ceil-

ing. In a corner, under the marble stairway, stood a
suit of armor.

I composed myself, remembering that the neighbors
might well be watching. "Ignacious? Are you in
there?"

There was no answer.

"Ignacious, I hope you don't mind if we come on
in. You don't, do you?"

Nobody forbade us to enter, so how could we not?
Wouldn't you, if you were in our size eleven shoes?
Mennonites eschew ostentation, and although I have
had very well-to-do guests stay at the inn, I seldom
get to see how the other half lives.

"Man, this is neat!" Susannah said. She was literally drooling.

"Careful of the parquet, dear," I said gently.

"Do you think he minds?"

"The door was unlocked, wasn't it? In Hernia that
might be the norm, but this is Bedford, remember?
They have crime here. I should think an unlocked
door here is an invitation to enter."

"I like the way you think, Mags."

Actually, I was equally torn between curiosity and
an almost paralyzing fear that I was going to end up
in the slammer for trespassing. I have been to jail, and
while I might look good in stripes, I would die if I
had to use an open toilet again. Susannah, however,
would feel right at home in the hoosegow. Her name
was carved on the walls of the Hernia jail. I've heard
rumors that the Bedford joint has a special bunk re-
served just for her.

We stepped inside, and I closed the door behind
me. I made it look as casual as if I lived there. This

was not an easy feat, considering I was shaking like a belly dancer on an ice floe.

"Dr. Pierce?" I called. "Are you home? Dr. Pierce?"

Except for the ticking of a mantel clock in the next room, the house was eerily silent.

"Maybe he's fallen and can't get up," Susannah said. "It wouldn't be right if we just ignored him."

I ignored her. "Dr. Pierce?" I called again. "Dr. Pierce?"

"Oh, Mags, you're such a wuss. We're already inside. What's it going to hurt if—damn!"

"Susannah! You know how I—oh, darn!"

Trust me, that's as bad as I swear. We both had a pretty good reason if you ask me. The miserable mongrel had managed to wiggle out of her bra and had leaped to the floor. Susannah tried to pounce on the pooch, but she misstepped and got hopelessly tangled in her own swirls. Fortunately she landed on the thick wool rug.

I tried to leap nimbly over her, but alas, I left my nimble days behind somewhere around my fortieth birthday. Fortunately I landed on the thick wool rug *and* Susannah.

Neither of us was seriously hurt, but by the time we got on our feet and had our bearings, the hound of Hades was halfway up the stairs. We chased after the beast.

"This time you're dog meat!" I shouted.

It was a wide stairs and we were able to climb side by side. I may have a decade on Susannah, but she has her clothes. Frankly, however, neither of us is fit. We huffed and puffed our way across a marble landing and were halfway up the second set when we simultaneously noticed the blood. It was dark, more black than red, and stood out sharply on the pale gray marble.

I looked up. At the head of the stairs was an arm, bent backward, and the top of someone's head. The hair was naturally red.

"Turn around," I ordered Susannah.

It was too late, she'd seen it too. And besides, it was impossible for either of us to do anything but keep on climbing.

"Don't look," I said.

We both stared. There, at the top of the stairs, lay the prone body of a man. He was lying on his stomach, his legs splayed. One arm was folded under him, the other, as I've said, extended over the edge of the stairs. Shnookums, that horrid creature, was sniffing the corpse as if it were a giant bowl of kibble.

And yes it was a corpse. I knew that without getting any closer. I've been around death enough to know that it has its own peculiar smell.

"Get the rat," I said quietly, "I'm calling 911."

Twenty

Florence Root's
World-Famous Peanut Brittle

◆

1 cup raw peanuts
1 cup sugar
½ cup white Karo syrup
¼ cup water
1 teaspoon baking soda

Mix sugar, syrup, and water in a saucepan. Cook on medium heat until mixture spins a "thread," stirring frequently. Add peanuts and cook until just barely brown (approximately seven minutes). Remove from heat. Add baking soda all at once and stir quickly. At this point the mixture will foam. Spread on a buttered cookie sheet and allow to cool. Break into pieces.

This is the lightest, tastiest peanut brittle in the entire world, and Wanda Hemphopple should be ashamed of herself for taking credit.

Twenty-one

The Bedford police could not have been kinder. Instead of hauling us off to the station and interrogating us under a naked lightbulb, they interviewed us in the dining room of the pseudo-Tudor, under a chandelier. Inspector Spratt, a mild-mannered man, perhaps in his mid-fifties, was in charge.

We were interviewed one at a time, first Susannah, and then myself. As a professional courtesy, they invited Susannah's husband, the incompetent Melvin Stoltzfus, to sit in on both interviews. I begged Inspector Spratt to pull out my fingernails instead. He merely laughed. I offered him my firstborn, should I ever have one. He declined. I seriously considered offering him the opportunity to see that there would be a firstborn, but alas, my morals are stronger than my instinct for self-preservation. Melvin stayed.

We took seats around one end of a massive mahogany table, me on one side, Melvin and Inspector Spratt on the other. Although I was so nervous my knees were playing a calypso tune, I couldn't help but admire the table. It was easily twice the size of the one I had back home. If my ancestor Jacob "The Strong" Yoder had seen such a table in his lifetime, he would have been so filled with envy and the desire to possess worldly things that he would have undoubtedly quit the Mennonite faith. It was a profound and sobering thought. Who knows what he might have become—a Baptist, or even a Presbyterian. Had there been but a larger table in eighteenth-century Hernia, I might well be sitting here in shorts, with painted nails and a mannish bob.

Inspector Spratt's gentle voice intruded on my reverie. "What were you doing inside the house of the victim?"

"Snooping," Stoltzfus snorted.

I gave him the evil eye. "Inspector Spratt asked *me,* dear." I turned to the detective. "I wanted to ask Dr. Pierce a question."

"What was the question?"

"Well, it's kind of complicated." I paused, to organize my thoughts.

Melvin jumped right in. "Everything you do is complicated, Yoder."

"You see," I wailed, "this man has it in for me!"

Inspector Spratt gave Melvin a meaningful look, but of course it was totally wasted. Insects aren't sensitive to human emotions, and besides, one of Melvin's mantis eyes was focused on the ceiling, the other at my face.

"Miss Yoder, take all the time you need to collect your thoughts. No one is trying to hurry you."

I took a deep breath. "Okay, here goes. Freni Hostetler, who is my cook, but also a cousin of sorts, has a daughter-in-law, Barbara, whom she despises. Only she doesn't despise her anymore because something came unstuck in Barbara's plumbing and she blossomed forth, as fertile as the Nile Valley."

"Give me a break," Melvin moaned.

"Please," the inspector said softly. "Continue, please, Miss Yoder."

"Well, not only did Barbara get pregnant, but she was all set to have triplets. In the meantime, however, Freni's husband Mose also got pregnant."

"Ha!"

Inspector Spratt and I both glared at Melvin. This time one of the wayward eyes must have made contact with the detective, because Melvin squirmed. Inspector Spratt nodded in my direction.

"He wasn't *really* pregnant, of course. He just had appendicitis. Anyway, the same time Barbara went into labor, Mose had an acute attack, and we had to rush them both to the hospital. To make a long story short, Mose ended up going to Bedford Memorial, but Barbara gave birth at Hernia Hospital, which hardly even counts as a hospital if you ask me."

"Which no one did," Melvin said.

"Enough," Spratt said curtly.

I gave Melvin a triumphant look, but I'm not sure if he caught it. "Well, now, where was I? Ah, yes. Dr. Bauer and Nurse Hemingway delivered the babies, but instead of triplets, there were only twins. Barbara and Jonathan—that's her husband—seemed to take it okay, but not Freni. She's sure that there really were three babies and that something happened to one."

"Like what?"

I shrugged. "I mean, it's not like the doctor or nurse could have just spirited one away. After all, Barbara and Jonathan were there the entire time. At any rate, Freni made me promise to investigate the situation, and even though it seemed a little silly to me at first, I went along. I spoke to both the doctor and the nurse, and they both stuck by the twins story. Then I started asking around—to other patients of Dr. Pierce—to see how competent he was. Maybe he made a mistake and counted wrong. Well, they thought he was a good doctor—at least they said they did. Of course, I would have spoken to Dr. Pierce directly, but it seems his office is closed. I did speak to his nurse, however, and she said he told her he'd suddenly decided to take a vacation."

"A permanent vacation," Melvin muttered, "thanks to you."

Inspector Spratt pushed back from the table and stood. I hadn't imagined he could look so stern.

"Chief Stoltzfus, please refrain from interrupting, or I will have to ask you to leave."

Melvin's mandibles mashed in agitation, but he said nothing. Spratt sat.

"Miss Yoder, when you arrived here, at the Pierce residence, was the front door unlocked?"

I nodded vigorously. "Yes, sir, it was. And I rang the doorbell lots of times. You can ask Susannah. Frankly, I don't know what made me actually try turning the knob, but aren't you glad now that I did?"

Spratt smiled. "Please, tell us exactly what you did when you found the door open."

I checked his ring finger. It was as bare as my left big toe. Not even a tan line. I doubted if he were a Mennonite—not with a funny name like Spratt—but we are always ready to welcome new believers.

"Well, we came in. I called Dr. Pierce's name, but of course he didn't answer. Then Susannah's dog got loose and—"

"Wait, please. Back up. What's this about a dog?"

Melvin turned the color of Freni's pickled beets. Who knew bugs could blush?

"My sister has a hideous little hound that goes everywhere with her. You wouldn't believe the places that mutt's been. Why, just today that itty-bitty beast burrowed in the biscuits, to say nothing of Wanda Hemphopple's beehive hairdo. But most of the time, you wouldn't know Shnookums was there. You see, my sister carries him around in her purse—well, actually, most of the time it's in her brassiere." It was my turn to blush, for having said the B word to a man.

Melvin groaned. From the sound of it, he was about to expire. I found this strangely exhilarating. The many times I have found myself fantasizing about Melvin's demise—it is a sin, I know that—I never once considered death by mortification. That opened a whole new realm of possibilities.

Inspector Spratt laughed. "I hope you don't mind me saying so, Miss Yoder, but you're a hoot."

"And a holler," I said, and then, remembering that fervid month following my faux nuptials, blushed again.

"Yeah, I just bet you are. Okay, now where were we?"

"I was about to describe how that loathsome rat leaped from my sister's bosom, and before we could stop him, he'd run upstairs. Of course we had to chase after him, and when we did we discovered Dr. Pierce's body. Believe me, we never would have set foot outside the foyer if it hadn't been for Melvin's dog."

"*My* dog?" It was amazing how fast Melvin could rally. It had taken but a microsecond for the mantis to go from mortified to mad.

"Well, he's your wife's dog, and what's *hers* is yours, right?"

Melvin knew exactly what I meant. Any inheritance

that couple hoped to come into was going to have to come from me, not Melvin's mother, who was a poor Mennonite farmer's widow.

"Right," he said sourly.

I turned to the inspector. "So when we found Melvin's dog sniffing at the corpse like it was a bowl of kibble, I called 911. That's why you'll find my fingerprints on the phone."

He nodded. "Well, that seems to do it for now. I assume I'll have no trouble reaching you at your inn?"

"I'm there night and day—well, normally. And here's my private number." I handed him a card. I'd show that Gabriel Rosen a thing or two. He might have a lover and baby stashed upstairs at his newly acquired farmhouse, but this gal has a few tricks stashed up her modest, elbow-length sleeves.

In a rare occurrence, both Melvin's eyes managed to focus on the same spot. In this case, Inspector Spratt's forehead. "You're letting her go? Just like that?"

Inspector Spratt smiled patiently. "She's answered all my questions."

"But she-she-she—" Melvin sputtered like a campfire in a drizzle.

I sailed regally out of the room. Proper exits are so important, don't you think? At any rate, I found Susannah in the foyer shamelessly flirting with a uniformed officer.

"You leaving with me? Or you leaving with *him*?"

Susannah winked at the young man in blue. "But I hardly know him."

"I meant your husband, dear. The man who once *mailed* his favorite aunt a carton of ice cream."

"But at least it was Rocky Road, her favorite flavor."

"Susannah!"

"All right. I'm coming with you. That is, if you'll drop me off at the Material Girl."

"The fabric store?"

"My sweetykins hates even going near that place, but Sergeant Walters here says they have some job openings."

Sergeant Walters cleared his throat. "My sister owns it."

I frowned. "That's a bit out of the way, and I've got a million things to do."

"Please, sis? You don't have to wait around. I'll hitch home from there."

"Okay, but just to drop you off."

I gave Susannah the lift she desired, and as promised, didn't stay. Naughty Eddy's Haircuts and More is located right next door to the Material Girl. Not only does Naughty Eddy live up to his name, but he seems to take a perverse pleasure in trying to get naughty with me. As for the safety issue, my baby sister has hitched to Alaska and back. Yes, I know, hitching can be very dangerous, but so can Susannah. She is, after all, armed with that dog.

I made a quick stop at Pat's I.G.A. in Bedford, and then drove straight home. I have a job after all. Being proprietress of the PennDutch Inn is a full-time occupation. It involves much more than just riding herd on a bunch of privileged folk who have more money than they can ever spend. Who do you think cleans the rooms of those folks who can't be talked into the A.L.P.O. plan? Seventy-five-year-old Freni? Sure, she helps, but I'm the one who hauls the equipment around, and does the grunt work. Besides, Freni is needed most in the kitchen.

It was almost noon when I parked my sinfully red BMW in the shade of a large maple and hightailed it in through the back door. I may not be the world's greatest cook, but that story about me burning water is just a rumor. And anyway, how hard can it be to cook those new frozen entrees Pat's been stocking lately? Anything to stop the Moregold twins from taking over my kitchen. Bubble and squeak indeed! That's all I did for the next two hours.

Much to my relief the kitchen was as empty as Aaron's heart the day he told me he already had a wife up in Minnesota. There were no pots on the stove, no smells wafting from one of two commercial size ovens.

"Thanks heavens!" I said aloud.

A second later I heard a faint thud. I wouldn't even have given it a second thought, had it not been followed by cries of distress. I flung the frozen entrees on the kitchen table and raced through the dining room and into the foyer. There, at the base of my impossibly steep stairs, lay Daphne Moregold.

Twenty-two

I gasped, but before I could run to her aid, Edwina Moregold came thundering down the stairs, a look of horror on her plump and usually placid face.

"Sis," she screamed, "are you all right?"

Daphne moaned.

"Sis, speak to me! How bad are you hurt?"

Daphne moaned again. I didn't hear any intelligible words, but apparently Edwina did.

"Your back? Did you say it's your back?"

"Yes, my back. Ooooooo."

At that point my heart, which had dropped into my stomach, was being rapidly devoured by gastric juices. This was not the first time I'd encountered a woman prone at the bottom of my stairs. Miss Brown, however, had been dead, and incapable of suing. What's more, she was already dead when someone threw her down the stairs.

I suppose a reasonable person might ask why, since a tornado demolished the original inn less than a year ago, I would go to the trouble to have a new set of impossibly steep stairs installed? The answer is simple: I'm sentimental. No, I'm not referring to Miss Brown, who resembled a burlap bag of potatoes when she literally hit bottom. I'm talking about the history of the inn. Its integrity, if you will. The inn is the site of my ancestral home, and it was those steep stairs—well, a set just like them—that generations of Yoders, Hostetlers, Kauffmans, and Masts used to get to the second-floor sleeping rooms. Why, once I even thought I saw the ghost of Grandma Yoder standing on those stairs, her face skewered into such a mean look of disapproval, for a second I thought she'd been resurrected from the dead.

One must keep in mind the elevator. Yes, it is rather small, and doesn't give the smoothest ride in the world, but it is there and available for all guests. And it is free. Therefore, I do not feel in the least bit responsible for those guests who elect to take the stairs. Still, I have a generous and comprehensive insurance policy just in case. Alas, this appeared as if it might be one of those cases.

"I'll call 911," I said generously. If my premiums skyrocketed, so be it.

Edwina looked startled. "What's that?"

"It's like an emergency rescue service. They'll get the hospital to send an ambulance out. They even dispatch the police if need be."

Before I could stop her, Daphne struggled to a sitting position. "There really is no need for that. I'll be all right."

"All the same, dear, you shouldn't move until a trained professional has seen you."

The twins exchanged glances. Then in a gesture that tugged at the strings of my rapidly shrinking heart, Edwina stroked her sister's hair.

"You see, Miss Yoder, we neglected to purchase travel insurance, and I'm not sure our U.K. insurance

plan covers us here. We operate on rather a different system."

"Still, your sister needs to be checked out. Tell you
what, I have a friend who is a doctor. He's a heart
doctor, but still he's a doctor. I'll give him a call and
see if he can come over and check you over. He lives
right across the road."

I would have thought the twins would have been
grateful—well, Daphne at least. Instead, they appeared annoyed.

"I can manage just fine," Daphne said. With Edwina's help she managed to stand. "A little bed rest is
all I'll be needing."

"Nonsense, dear. I'll have Dr. Rosen over here in
a jiffy."

"Really, I'm quite fine." Daphne took a small step
forward and winced.

"You see? You're not fine. You're in pain. Now
don't move a muscle." I ran to the phone.

Heaven only knows what Gabe was up to, and why
it took him so long to answer. I was beginning to think
he wasn't home, or worse yet, up to no good with the
mother of that baby I'd heard. But, and this is based
on personal experience, even *that* shouldn't take more
than the equivalent of ten rings.

"Rosen here," he finally said.

"Well, it's about time, dear," I said crossly. "I
thought New Yorkers were known for their speed."

"What?"

"As in a New York minute. Obviously you were
raised elsewhere."

"Actually, I was raised in Manhattan. But I was

born in Bridgeport, Connecticut. Perhaps that makes the difference."

"You're making fun of me, aren't you?"

"I was just teasing a little. But I really was born in Bridgeport. Moved to Manhattan when I was three."

"That's nice, dear, but I have a situation over here. I could use your help."

"What kind of situation?"

"A woman fell."

In the ensuing silence lasting peace came to the Middle East, and Calista Flockhart gained fifty pounds.

"Fell?" he echoed finally. "How?"

"I didn't do it, if that's what you mean! But she claims to have fallen down my stairs."

"And what exactly do you want me to do?"

"Why, check her out of course."

"Magdalena, I'm a cardiologist, and a nonpracticing one at that."

"I don't know about New York City, but here in these parts neighbors help each other out."

"Well, I'm all for helping a neighbor out, but this sounds more like an official doctor's visit."

"Who said anything about official, dear? I wasn't planning to pay you."

He laughed. "You're really something, you know that?"

"Yeah, I'm a scream."

As if on cue that darn baby started crying in the background. *It* again! I'd been trying to block that infant out of my mind, because where there's a baby, there most often is a mother. Although at one point in our fledgling relationship Gabe had stated, in no uncertain terms, that he was unattached, that didn't necessarily mean that was the case. Just look at Aaron, to whom I had offered the flower of my womanhood. Just a month later I had nothing to show for it but potpourri and a broken heart. Men are capable of lying, you know. Besides, I have ears that can hear corn grow, and I know what I heard.

"What's that noise?" I demanded.

"What noise?"

"Don't play games with me, buster. It's a baby, isn't it?"

"In a manner of speaking."

"And I suppose its mother is there as well? In a manner of speaking?"

"No. I've never seen her mother."

Her? Then an awful thought crossed my mind.

"Just whose baby is it, and where did you get her?"

"For the moment that's my business. But if it will make you feel better, I acquired her legitimately."

"Is that so? When did you get her?"

"Yesterday."

I gasped. "Yesterday!"

"Is there an echo on this line?"

Be calm, I told myself. You owe it to Freni and Barbara to not let your feelings for this man get in the way of clear thinking.

"How old is your baby?"

"Eight weeks."

"Eight weeks?" Even a doctor couldn't pass an eight-week-old baby off as a newborn. Still, I've read in the newspaper where folks have tried things just as stupid. There is the true case of an Ohio woman who kidnapped a newborn boy from the hospital, took him home, and then called paramedics and claimed she had just given birth. It was one thing for the kidnapper to try to explain the neatly tied umbilical chord, but even the dullest paramedic knows that babies are not born circumcised.

"Two months is what I said."

"Can you prove that?"

"As a matter of fact I can."

"Why haven't you mentioned this baby before?"

"It was meant to be a surprise."

"For whom?"

"I'll be right over."

"Don't do me any favors," I snapped.

He hung up before I could.

When I got back to the Moregold sisters, Daphne was sitting, eyes closed, on the first step. Edwina was sitting beside her sister, her arm around the woman. They both looked like they'd had the joie de vivre knocked right out of them.

"You took an awfully long time on the telephone," Edwina said quietly. A more sensitive soul might have heard accusation in her voice.

I gave her a warning look. "How's the patient?"

Daphne opened one eye. "I've been better. Perhaps you and sis could help me into the lift now. If I could just lie down on my bed, I'm sure it would help a lot."

I reluctantly helped Daphne upstairs and into bed. She moaned and groaned the entire time. I hadn't heard such pitiful sounds since that day, back in the fifties, when Mama leaned too close to our new washer, the one with an electric clothes wringer, and inadvertently invented the mammogram. At any rate, it seemed to me that the best thing would have been for Daphne to not move, at *all*, until Gabe had examined her. But what do I know? I'm just a lowly inn-keeper on the wrong side of the big pond.

Wouldn't you know that in helping her sister get into bed, Edwina threw her back out too?

"You what?" I wailed.

It was Edwina's turn to moan and groan while Daphne explained.

"It happens to us all the time. It's because we're identical twins."

"You throw your backs out all the time?"

"No, this is the first time for backs. But you see, because we're identical twins, most likely when one of us comes down with something, the other will too."

"But sprained backs aren't communicable."

"Of course they're not. But sis and I are essentially the same person. We come from the same egg, after all. Our karmas are connected."

Fortunately the doorbell rang. Just to be on the safe side, in case bad backs—or more likely bad luck—were contagious, I took the elevator down. The model I chose was one of the cheaper ones, and if I should even suffer an accident in it, my next bed will be in heaven.

The doorbell rang again, and again before I could answer it.

"Hold your horses," I said as I flung it open.

There stood Gabe, a foolish grin across his other-wise handsome face. He was holding what at first looked like a mailbox. You know, the kind set on poles in rural areas. Shaped like a bread box, only bigger. This one, however, didn't have an arched top, and the lid was wire mesh.

"That's an odd-looking medical bag, Doctor."

The grin widened. "It's not my medical bag. It's your baby."

"Little Freni?"

"She's all yours. Name her what you want."

I grabbed the stupid-looking box from him and peered inside. "But that's a kitten!"

"A Siamese kitten. A pure-blooded Chocolate Point. She's got papers and everything."

I staggered into the house, not from the weight of the box, but from a curious mixture of relief and bitter disappointment. Had there been a Hostetler baby in the box, it would have meant a successful, if somewhat bizarre end to my search. But I was relieved nonetheless, because the baby I had heard crying was not the product of Gabe's loins. Not in this life.

"So this is what was making all that noise."

He nodded. "Siamese cats are notorious for sounding like human infants."

"Why didn't you tell me? And why the kitten for me?" Meanwhile the kitten had stuck a little leg through the grid and was trying to bat at my hand.

"What's today?" Gabe asked.

I frowned at his delaying tactic. "Tuesday."

"What's the date?"

"July twenty-third."

"So?"

"So a needle pulling thread?" I don't listen to much worldly music, but that particular song has good Mennonite lyrics.

"So, tomorrow is our anniversary. I was going to give you the kitten then, but you made it clear you couldn't wait."

"What?"

"Face it, Magdalena, you were throwing a hissy fit. Pun intended."

I waved aside the accusation. "*Which* anniversary would this be?"

"Why, our three-month anniversary, of course."

I stared at Gabe, my mouth open so wide, I could well have choked on a wayward robin. He was right. We had indeed met in April. I remembered that because of Susannah's wedding. I had just met Gabe and invited him as my guest. But I for one hadn't kept track of the exact date. But Gabe had! How terribly romantic! Aaron's idea of romance had been to take off his socks before he came to bed.

"Uh—uh—of course, our three-month anniversary."

"Well?"

"Well, your present isn't quite ready," I wailed. "After all, you did say it was tomorrow."

"What I meant was, how do you like your present? Little Freni is what you named her, right?"

At that very moment the kitten was successful in batting my hand. She did so with a full set of untrimmed claws. I yelped and nearly dropped the carrier.

"She wants out. Let her out, Magdalena. Let her get to know you."

What fools we were: he wanting to impress me with a gift, and me in such shock at receiving it that neither of us had a thought for those two poor bedridden gals upstairs. Oh, well, such is love—not that we were in love, mind you, but perhaps the barest beginnings of love. In deep like, as it were.

I let Freni out of her cage. Unlike her namesake, she was a lithe and beautiful creature. Pale cream body, chocolate face and ears, chocolate boots, and a chocolate tail. Her eyes were even bluer than Aaron's had been. She rubbed against my ankles and purred.

I bent to pet her. "Ooh, youms is so sweet," I heard myself say. "Yes, you is, yes, you is."

Little Freni purred louder, sounding for all the world like Big Freni did when she snored. I petted some more, and she purred even louder. Then suddenly, in the throes of her purring frenzy, Little Freni snagged the front of my dress with her claws, and before I could stop her, climbed up the front panel, all the way to the top button. Hesitating only a second or two, she poked her pink nose under the collar facing and crawled in, straight into my gaping bra cup. A quick tickling turn, and she was settled in, her left ear barely noticeable above the V of my neckline. And lest you think there is no room in a bra for an eight-week-old kitten—well, there is, *if* you forget to use tissues that day.

"Of course if you don't like her," Gabe said, "I could always take her back."

"Do so and die," I said. The tragedy is, I only half meant it. I realize that owning a kitten doesn't make one a full-fledged mother, but I had never felt such strong maternal feelings, not even toward Susannah. Now here I was, the product of five hundred years of pacifist inbreeding, suddenly willing—well, half willing—to turn my back on a noble heritage, and for what? To keep a *cat*?

Gabe laughed. "You're beautiful, you know that?"

"Who's beautiful? Little Freni or me?"

A loud thump from upstairs made me wait for my answer.

Twenty-three

I raced up my impossibly steep stairs, quite forgetting there was a hitchhiker in my bra. Gabe, whose motivation lacked lawsuits, followed at a somewhat slower pace.

"What happened?" I demanded. Although I could see quite well what had happened. There, lying on their respective single beds, were the Moregold twins. Between their beds, laying facedown, was the small bureau, which doubles as a nightstand. Thank heavens its drawers always stick. Otherwise there might well be unmentionables scattered about.

"We had to get your attention," Edwina said calmly. "We called and called, but you didn't answer."

"So you turned over the bureau?"

"It took both our efforts," Daphne said. "And it didn't make our backs any better."

Edwina pointed to the bed, where a lamp lay beside her. "At least we removed the lamp first."

I shook my head in disbelief. "I was gone only ten minutes."

"Well, it seemed like forever."

"Besides, we were getting thirsty," Edwina said.

"*What?*"

"A glass of lemonade would be nice."

"I'd prefer a beer," Daphne said. "But not cold, like you Americans drink it. Of course we wouldn't dream of being a bother, so if it won't be too long, you can bring our drinks up with lunch."

"Lunch?"

"Oh, nothing fancy, mind you. Perhaps a little chicken salad. Our auntie, Ms. Virginia Wilcox, makes the best chicken salad. It has nectarines."

"Is that all you want? You sure you don't want some toad stroganoff?"

Daphne had the audacity to roll her eyes. "I think she means toad-in-the-hole."

"I meant what I said." And I did. Great Granny Yoder didn't have a drop of English blood, British or otherwise, nonetheless she managed to invent a rather tasty dish and name it after amphibians.

The twins exchanged glances. "I'll give it a go," Edwina said at last. "But make mine a small portion."

I jiggled a pinkie in both ears just to make sure nothing was blocked, and that they were working right. "You women are serious, aren't you? You really expect me to serve you lunch in bed?"

The normally ebullient twins frowned in tandem. "Well, we obviously can't go downstairs," Edwina said.

I put my hands on my hips, a distinctly un-Mennonite gesture. "Is that so? Well, we'll just see what the doctor has to say. And as for that beer, I'm telling you right now, a Presbyterian has a better chance of getting into heaven than you do getting one sip of the devil's brew under this roof."

"Then make it two lemonades," Daphne said.

"Why I never!"

Gabe stepped into the room. He must have been

waiting in the hallway, because when Daphne saw
him, her eyes bulged, big as scones.

"Ooh, sis. Check out the doc. We don't have nothing like him back home in National Health Care."

"Down, girl," I said. "Down, you little beast." I
actually was talking to Little Freni, who had decided
to try my other cup, but if Daphne wanted to believe
my remarks were directed to her, so be it.

Edwina put the lamp on the floor and patted the
bed beside her. "You can sit here, Doctor."

"But I saw him first," Daphne whined.

"Yes, but you told me to check him out." Edwina
looked Gabe straight in the eye. "Should we disrobe
for the exam?"

"You crumpet-eating strumpet!" I railed. "This man
is mine. If anyone gets to disrobe, it's me. Only I
won't, because we're not married. Not that we never
will be, mind you, but then it's far too early in our
relationship to even consider that. But we do have a
relationship, you know. Look, he gave me this." I
tugged on my dress collar to give the gals a peek at
Little Freni.

Edwina smirked. "He gave you a hairy chest?"

Gabe laughed, but at least he didn't dispute my
claim. "Ladies, please. There will be no need for anyone to disrobe." He turned to me. "Magdalena, would
you please go downstairs and get my bag. I left it on
the front porch."

I retrieved the bag, and even though Gabe kept the
door wide open during his examination, he made me
wait outside. During my exile the Charlotte Panthers
won a game, and Dennis Rodman grew up. But I
caught glimpses now and then—both women remained
fully clothed—and although I couldn't hear most of

what Gabe said, I think he behaved professionally. There was, however, far too much giggling from the girls.

At one point, out of sheer boredom, I wandered down the hall to Room 6, where my mystery guest was staying. "Jacko," I whispered softly, "it's me, Magdalena."

There was no answer.

I drummed lightly on the door with my fingertips. "I've been very patient, dear. Either you show yourself, or I charge you full fare this time."

The door opened a crack and I peered in. The figure in black was far too large to be Michael Jackson.

"Why, you're not Jacko, after all."

"No, ma'am."

"Then who are you?"

"The King."

"Charlie Windsor?" I knew that man too. "Give it up, dear. There wouldn't be room for those royal ears under that ski mask of yours. Besides, the queen is still alive. You'd only be the Prince of Wales."

"No, ma'am, I'm not that king. I'm *The* King."

"Elvis?"

"Shhhh."

"Get out of town! Elvis Presley is dead."

"Ma'am, I'm afraid rumors of my death have been greatly exaggerated."

"Mark Twain is dead too. Look, buster, whoever you are, you better make good on your bill."

"Just a minute," he mumbled. In less than sixty seconds he thrust a cloth bag through the crack. "Here, take what you need."

"How many days' stay?"

"Six."

I rummaged through the bag until I had the right amount. No doubt this sounds dangerous and foolish to you, but as the owner of an inn that caters to celebrities—well, it used to, before the tornado—I'd been through this many times. Half of Hollywood has recovered from the surgeon's knife under my roof. What better place to go to heal than Hernia? The Amish don't care about movie and television stars, and frankly, those Mennonites who do are not very savvy. Lodema Schrock, who watches far more television than a pastor's wife should admit to, used to rave about a show with a talking horse. This Ed—or Ned, maybe—was a real horse, Lodema claimed. She could see his lips move. No amount of persuasion could convince the woman that the beast in question was really a puppet. You see what I mean?

"Look, dear—whoever you are—I've got a lot on my plate at the moment. If you want anything on *your* plate, you're going to have to show up for meals. I can't be bothered bringing up trays."

The ski mask nodded.

At that moment Gabe joined me in the hallway. "Can we talk?" he whispered.

I motioned him to follow me downstairs. The masked man closed his door.

"How are they?" I demanded when we were back in the foyer.

He shrugged. "They appear to be in good health."

"Both of them?"

"Yes. But back pain is a very difficult thing to prove, or disprove. I tried talking them into going for some X rays, but they refused."

"So, now what?"

"Well, that's your call. Frankly, Magdalena, I don't

think either of them is having trouble with their backs. The trouble is more in their heads."

"They're crazy?"

"Crafty is more like it. From what I could gather they've had a hard life—"

"Who hasn't?" I wailed.

"Touché. But these ladies both work in dead-end factory jobs and share a cold-water flat in the grimiest neighborhood of one of England's largest industrial cities. They've been saving their meager salaries for years just to come to America, and when they finally do, they discover Nirvana."

"The rock group?"

"No, the PennDutch Inn."

"Come again?"

"They love it here, Magdalena. And they adore you."

"They do?"

"Absolutely. You're the kind of mother they wish they would have had."

"I'm not that old!"

"You know what I mean."

"Yes, but at first they were so helpful. They pitched right in and made meals without being told. But now they want to be served beer in bed?"

He laughed. "That was cheeky of Daphne. But you see, they've decided they like it here so much—at the inn, with you—that they don't want to leave. So they've taken to their beds with bogus back pains. Only I can't prove it. And as a doctor I shouldn't make such a prognosis without more tests. But there you have it. That's my gut feeling."

"But I offered Disney World!"

"Yes, but they couldn't be sure of liking that. You, they already do."

I wrung my hands. They really are attractive hands, if I must say so myself.

"You haven't answered my question, Gabe. What do I do now?"

"That's the tricky part. The possibility for strained muscles does exist. At least for Daphne. But speaking as your friend, and not a physician, I'd say the thing to do would be to somehow make them not like you."

"How do I do that?" I may have a tart tongue, and hold more opinions than a Gallup poll, but in general, people like me. There are a few misguided souls, like Lodema Schrock, our pastor's wife, who can't abide me, but folks like her are few and far between. Perhaps I could ask her for tips.

Gabe spread his heads. And they are very handsome hands too, if I might add.

"You might try ignoring them."

"Would that work?"

"I'd say it's worth a shot. I mean, you do have certain rules here, don't you?"

"You can say that again! I simply will not tolerate anyone being late for meals." I hung my head. "Unless it's me who's late."

"There you go. Tell the twins they've missed the magical hour and they're out of luck."

"They aren't the only ones," I said. Here it was, almost one o'clock on a Tuesday, and I had yet to see that nice Mennonite couple, the Redigers, or the rich vamp Vivian Mays and her gold-digging boy-toy. Although the latter was no surprise.

From where he was standing in the foyer Gabe could see both into the parlor, which was on his left, and the dining room on his right. "It does seem to be pretty dead around here, doesn't it?"

"You're telling me. Not that I'm complaining," I said quickly. "I've had a lot on my plate with this wild goose chase Freni's sent me on, not to mention the murder this morning."

Gabe grabbed my arm. "What murder?"

"Up in Bedford. Susannah and I stumbled across a body."

"Oh, Magdalena. Do you want to talk about it?"

I let Gabe lead me to a Victorian loveseat in the parlor. Frankly, that particular piece of furniture is not in the least bit comfortable, and does not inspire thoughts of love. It was, however, just the right place for us to sit and talk about my day.

"You're really something," Gabe said when I was quite through.

"Yeah, I know."

"You're a damn fool, that's what you are."

"I beg your pardon?"

"You have a perfectly good life right here, being an innkeeper. Why the hell do you insist on subjecting yourself to all kinds of danger?"

"*Excuse* me?"

"Don't you know you could have been killed? The murderer could still have been there someplace, hiding in the house."

"Well, it's not like we expected to find a corpse."

"Yes, but you stayed there until the police came. *Inside* the house."

"True, but the police *were* coming. We knew that. Besides, Dr. Pierce had been dead for hours."

"How could you tell?"

"I've been around dead bodies before, that's how."

"I see. So you're an expert, are you?"

His hand was still on my arm. I wrenched free and stood.

"Look, I don't tell you how to lead your life. You have no business telling me how to lead mine."

He stood as well. "I'm not trying to be controlling, if that's what you think."

"I didn't say that." But that's exactly how I felt. It had occurred to me that the kitten snuggled next to my scrawny chest was not a considerate gift. One should not give animals as gifts without first consulting the recipient. The cuddly kitten would soon outgrow even my lingerie, and then what? If I didn't have it declawed, it would shred my furniture. If I didn't get it spayed, I'd find myself grandmother to dozens of little mixed breed kittens I couldn't give away. And either I kept the poor thing outside in the elements, or I could devote a good five minutes a day sifting through a litter box and sweeping scatter. A cat was also a long-term commitment. A well-cared-for feline could live twenty years or more. I could be ready to retire well before Little Freni was ready to expire. Then what would I do? Pay expensive kenneling bills if I wanted to travel? In retrospect, Gabe's gift was not quite the romantic gesture it had at first seemed to be.

"Well, what were you thinking right now?" Gabe demanded. "You seemed lost in space."

"I was thinking that you should have asked before saddling me with a twenty-year responsibility."

His face darkened. "Oh, so you want to give her back?"

I glanced down into the nether reaches of my bosom. Little Freni had fallen fast asleep, her head now on her paws. A casual observer would not even have been able to tell there was a pussy hidden somewhere beneath my clothes.

"No, I don't want to give her back. But I do want you to pay to have her spayed."

"Fair enough."

"And next time, ask before giving me a pet."

He smiled. "You'll have to forgive me for being so impetuous and emotional. I guess it's the writer in me."

"You were also a cardiologist, dear. Heaven help your patients."

"Amen to that."

"Are you making fun of my religion?"

"Not at all. Hey, maybe I better get going before I lose any more ground today."

I said nothing.

"Well then, good-bye."

"Good-bye," I said. "And thank you for the gift." But I didn't walk him to the door.

"Welcome to the PennDutch," I said to Little Freni.

She purred in her sleep, while I gazed through the front door at a shrinking Gabe. He had a nice backside, I'll say that much.

"Just as soon as I get a few loose ends tied up, we're off to Sam Yoder's. I suppose you'll be needing some kitten chow. And then there's the matter of your litter box. You do use one, don't you? I mean, you do at least understand that a good kitty doesn't soil her bed, right?"

"Miss Yoder!" It was a fairly faint call, coming as it was from upstairs, but I jumped nonetheless. Heaven forfend anyone should catch me talking to my dress.

"Not now, dears!" I hollered. "I'm busy!"

"Miss Yoder! Oh, Miss Yoder. We've been waiting on those lemonades." It sounded like Daphne.

"And lunch!" That must have been Edwina.

"You'll find what you need in the kitchen," I yelled pleasantly.

"But our backs!" they wailed in unison.

"Yes, dears, I'll be back!"

I trotted off to my room, which is on the first floor at the back of the house, as far away from the open stairs as one could get. I took the phone from the lobby, so I could make my phone calls in there.

Mandilla Gindlesperger's telephone was answered on the first ring. "Chad, is that you?"

"It most certainly is not!"

"Come on, Chad, I recognize your voice. Be you've been sucking on them balloons again, haven't you? Your voice is still a little high." The speaker was, without a doubt, a teenybopper. She popped gum when she spoke, a habit I find even more annoying than a raised toilet seat.

"This is Magdalena Yoder, young lady. I want to speak to your mother."

"Good one, Chad. Hey, you're not supposed to call here. If Mama finds out she'll kill me."

"Put your mama on the phone!" I barked.

"Funny, Chad. Look, why don't I just meet you at our secret spot? Like in an hour, okay? I'm supposed to be washing lunch dishes right now."

When in Rome, do like the Romans, right? When accused of being a teenage boy, act like one!

"Hey, baby, I got us a new spot to meet," I said speaking in my lowest register. "How about in front of Yoder's Corner Market?"

"You're kidding! Man, that's way cool. Since we just got busted last week for swiping smokes. Mama will never think to look for us there."

"Yeah, but I got an even better idea. You wait for me at our usual spot, and I'll swipe the smokes. Then if something goes wrong, we both won't get busted."

"Oh, man, but I hate waiting in that old church by myself."

"Why?"

There are some conversations we are meant to have, and this was one of them. I firmly believe it was the Good Lord's plan that I call Mandilla, and chose to dial exactly when I did.

"Why? Don't be so ignorant, Chad. That place is haunted, and you know that. You heard that organ playing. We ran upstairs, remember? Only there was no one there."

That had to be the First Mennonite Church on North Elm Street. That's not my church, but a more liberal representative of my denomination, and the site of Hernia's most famous ghost story. The story goes that the church's first organist—the pastor's wife—suffered a heart attack while practicing alone one Saturday afternoon. Since then there have been numerous reports of congregants, and even just casual passersby, hearing beautiful, but sad music when the church was locked and empty.

I made a few pitiful hen noises. "Hey, y'ain't getting chicken on me, are ya?"

The teenybopper sighed. "Course not. I'll be in the basement, like always. But I hate squeezing through that little window. And this time I'm taking a flashlight along—just in case the lights go out."

"You do that, dear." I spoke in my highest, clearest, most Magdalena tones.

"Hey, what the fudge?" Actually, the girl used a dirty word I would never repeat. "You ain't Chad, are you?"

"I'm afraid not, dear. I'm Magdalena Yoder, like I said."

"Oh, man! Busted already and I ain't even left the house!"

"Well, you win some, I guess, and you lose some. You just lost big time, dear, but there are a couple of things you can do to make it easier on yourself."

"Yeah? Name them!"

Twenty-four

"**Y**ou can tell on yourself."

"Sugar!" she said—well, not that word either, but you get my drift. "Why the hell would I want to do that?"

"Because that way you get to choose exactly how and when. If I tell her, it will be within the next couple of minutes, and I don't like little girls who sneak around and lie to their parents. In fact, I don't particularly like little girls at all."

"I ain't a little girl!"

"Well, I'm not too fond of most big girls either. So, are you going to do it?"

"Man, that would be ratting out Chad."

"That may well be, but speaking of rats, I'm a bigger rat than you or Chad put together. You don't want to mess with me."

Gum cracked, but she said nothing.

"Well?"

"Okay, but I don't have to like it!"

"That is for sure. But you will do it, and before you see Chad again. And I want your mama to call me to let me know that she knows."

"Oh, man!" There was series of staccato gum pops. "Is that the two things?"

"I beg your pardon?"

"You said there was a couple of things I had to do to make it easier."

"Right. But that was just one thing. The second thing is, I want you to put your mother on the phone."

"But you said you wouldn't tell!" The teenybopper, whose name I still didn't know, had all but broken my eardrum. Little Freni woke, mewed once, and then mercifully went back to sleep. It's hard to say who had more powerful lungs, the kitten or the teenybopper.

"What was that noise?" the teenybopper demanded.

"Never you mind. Now, about your mama . . . I won't tell her. This is a different matter altogether. Now get her on the phone."

"Oh, man!"

"Now!"

"Okay, okay. You don't have to get so bent out of shape. Geez!"

The receiver on her end smacked against something and I jerked it away from my ear. Then I waited. During the ensuing silence Hillary dumped Bill and the national debt all but disappeared. If Mandilla didn't get on the line soon, Little Freni was going to need that litter box before I could get to the store. Finally, when I had all but despaired of speaking to the woman, and had in fact organized a gray hair-counting contest with several of myselves in front of the bedroom mirror, Mandilla got on the line.

"Debbie told me everything," were the first words out of her mouth.

"Come again?"

"She told me about her meetings with Chad in the church basement. And stealing the cigarettes. I didn't know any of that was happening. Honest."

"I believe you," I said. "But that's really not why I called."

"This whole time I thought she was spending her days at her sister's house. I want you to know, Magdalena, that I'm not going to let her get away with it. I'm going to give her what for."

"At least she told you, dear. I hope you give her credit for that."

"We're a good Christian family, Magdalena. I won't tolerate what she and Chad were doing in that church." She sighed. "Although I guess I should be grateful they stole condoms along with the cigarettes."

"Spare me the details, dear. I really did call about another matter."

"Oh?" She seemed to be in a fog.

"It's about that wonderful thing you're doing, giving your next baby to God. I've been thinking a lot about that. Just how does one go about doing that?"

She gasped. "Oh, Magdalena, you're not—why, you're not even married."

"I'm not pregnant," I wailed. "But what if I was?"

"Don't be ridiculous! The Lord despises unwed mothers."

"What about the Virgin Mary?"

"And now you blaspheme!"

I sighed. There is no arguing theology with a woman whose church has thirty-two words in its name.

"Okay, so it isn't me. I just wanted to know how *you* plan to go about it. Will you just leave the baby at church?"

"Of course not!"

"Well, then how? Please share."

Mandilla's sigh blew candles out as far away as Bedford. "All right. But only because you did me a favor

by telling me what my Debbie was up to. You see,
it's like this. The day I learned I was pregnant with
this one, I started praying mightily. Levi doesn't make
that much money working as dishwasher at the Sausage Barn and—"

"Your husband works at the Sausage Barn?"

"Are you being judgmental, Magdalena?"

"Absolutely not, dear." Sometimes it is okay to
bend the truth so as not to hurt the feelings of others.
It may not be in the Bible, but if the most powerful
man in the world does it, can it be so bad?

"Because who are you to talk? You think just because you charge fancy prices, you're not still in the
service industry? If that's the case, I have news for
you—you are! My Levi buses tables and washes
dishes, but he doesn't clean toilets. Just because Brad
Pitt pooped in your pot doesn't make your toilet any
less dirty."

She had a point there. "I take it that what you were
trying to say is that the Sausage Barn and Miller's
Feed Store, even together, don't pay a livable wage."

"Exactly. And although most of our kids are old
enough to have some kind of a job, well—Hernia
doesn't exactly abound witn opportunities." She
paused to let her point sink in.

I swallowed. The summer before a Gindlesperger
boy had stopped by the PennDutch asking for odd
jobs, but I'd turned him down. Yes, I know it's unfair
to discriminate against someone just because his
mother sat on my lunch bag thirty years earlier, but
there you have it. Contrary to any rumors you may
have heard, I am far from perfect.

"Go on, dear. So you prayed for financial assistance, right?"

"Yes. *'Ask and ye shall receive'*—Matthew seven, verse seven. So I asked. I was expecting maybe Levi would get a raise, but like the Bible says, the Lord works in mysterious ways."

"How so in this case?"

"Well, Levi was talking to one of the customers— one he'd never seen before—and suddenly this guy says—'Brother, the Lord hath sent me to you. The child in thy wife's womb hath been claimed by Jehovah.' "

"Get out of town!"

"Magdalena, do you want to hear this or not?"

"I do, I do!"

"Then hold thy tongue," she said, lapsing into Biblese, and then just as quickly out again. "So anyway, you can imagine that poor Levi was freaked out by all of this, but the customer says, 'Fear not, all shall be well. Thy seed shall prosper. Verily, the fruit of Mandilla's womb shall stand before the nations, and all the nations of the earth shall bow before him like sheaves of wheat.' "

I bit my tongue and slapped both cheeks, so as not to say anything sarcastic. It was a lost cause.

"Really, dear, this is too—"

"Good to be true? But such are the ways of Jehovah." She paused. "Say hallelujah."

"What?"

"Say hallelujah."

"Hallelujah!"

"Was that a sarcastic hallelujah?"

"Heavens no. Please continue, dear."

"Okay. Now where was I?"

"The United Nations was going to bow before you like barley loaves."

"That was wheat sheaves. But, yes. And then this messenger went on to tell Levi that we were to name the child Samuel—because of course it is to be a boy—and that the Lord wants us to turn him over as soon as possible after birth." She sighed deeply. "Apparently this is so there will be no chance for us to taint Samuel with the ways of the world. Magdalena, do you think Levi and I would taint the child?"

"Ours is not to question why, ours is but to do and die," I said, mangling a line from *Charge of the Light Brigade,* and immediately regretting it.

"Exactly. And it's a great honor to have the Lord God Jehovah request the fruit of one's loom."

"You mean loins, don't you, dear?"

"Magdalena, must you always interrupt?"

"Pretty much. That seems to be my nature. So tell me, dear, what do you do once little Samuel is born? Drop him off at the Sausage Barn?"

"As a matter of fact, yes."

"Is that legal?"

"Magdalena, don't ever underestimate the power of the Almighty. The messenger just happens to be a lawyer."

"Surprise!"

"What's that supposed to mean?"

"Nothing, dear. I was just surprised that angels went to law school. I didn't know there were sharks in heaven." Pigs maybe, but surely not sharks.

"I didn't say that messenger was an angel—although—and this gives me the goose bumps just to think it—maybe he is."

"So, it's a he?"

"Of course, Magdalena!"

My heart raced. "Was he a short little man with

white hair and thick glasses? Oh, and a handlebar mustache?"

"Don't be ridiculous. He was comely, like a proper angel. You really should read your Bible more."

"I'll take that under advisement. Did he have a name?"

"Of course. His name was Donald."

"*Donald?* As in duck?"

"Jehovah will not abide mocking, Magdalena. It says so in that unread Bible of yours."

"I read it every day! And there's nothing in the Bible about an angel named Donald."

"Well, perhaps Donald is the Hebrew form."

I very much doubted that. "Well, at any rate, you really believe this customer was sent from God?"

"It's clear, Magdalena. He is the answer to all our prayers. Not only will our little Samuel grow up to serve the Lord—which is an honor and a blessing just in itself, but the Lord is blessing us financially as well."

"How so?"

"The Lord has seen fit to give us ten thousand dollars for the privilege of giving back to Him what was His to begin with."

"God pays for babies?"

"Magdalena, you are a woman of such little faith."

"I most certainly am not!" I have a great deal of faith—well, okay, a great deal of doubt too. According to Reverend Schrock, we all do. It's just I don't think the Good Lord goes around bankrolling baby adoptions.

"You know, Magdalena, you're welcome to come with me to my church."

"The First and Only True Church of the One and Only Living God of the Tabernacle of the Supreme

Holiness and Healing and Keeper of the Consecrated Righteousness of the Eternal Fire of Jehovah?" I said it in one breath.

"That's Flame, not Fire, and I think you're making fun of me."

"Well, you have to admit it is an awfully long name."

"There's much more to a church than its name. Worship begins at nine sharp. Do you want me to pick you up, or can you make it on your own?"

"I don't need a ride," I said honestly.

"Good, because Samuel has dropped."

"I beg your pardon?"

"He's assuming the birth position. I know these things, Magdalena. I've been through it many times. Our gift to the Lord will be born any day now."

I sensed the conversation was about to end. "Look, dear, before you hand little Samuel over, you might want to get that financial blessing you have coming in your hot little hands. And if I were you, I'd make sure it was in cash. Heaven is a long way to go to make good on a bounced check."

She hung up.

Twenty-five

Ms. Virginia Wilcox's
Chicken Nectarine Salad

◆

(I did *not* serve this to the demanding Moregold twins)

3 cups cooked chicken
1½ cups sliced celery
3 nectarines, sliced
1½ cups dark sweet cherries
1 tablespoon sliced green
   onions
½ cup toasted almonds

Dressing:

1 cup mayonnaise
2 tablespoons vinegar
2 tablespoons honey
1 teaspoon lime juice

½ teaspoon curry powder
¼ teaspoon salt

Toss all ingredients except for almonds. Sprinkle almonds on top and serve.
Serves eight.

Twenty-six

Little Freni made it quite clear she couldn't hold out until I had a chance to buy litter. Fortunately I have a huge potted geranium on the front porch. Actually, only the pot is large. The geranium itself is a spindly collection of half-shriveled, almost-leafless stems. I know potted plants need to be watered from time to time, but a life like mine makes ornamental horticulture a low priority. At any rate, the soil in the pot was lose, and relatively free of parasites. Little Freni was more than willing to make that her pit stop.

"You good to go, dear?"

The kitten meowed confirmation, so I plucked my petite pussy from the pot and tucked her back in my bra. Of course I got potting soil down my bosom, but that comes with the territory of being a new mother. At least there were no diapers to wash.

We headed out to the Zook farm. It's in the opposite direction of Sam Yoder's Corner Market, but my potted geranium had bought me some time. And since what comes out must first go in, I had thoughtfully brought along a small zip-top can of chunk white tuna I found in the pantry.

This time there was a good deal more visible activity going on at the Zook spread. Two small boys, one towheaded, one dark, were playing with a large, partially deflated ball on the front lawn. The bespectacled grandmother was sitting on the front porch, her gnarled hands folded on the apron of her lap. She appeared to be asleep. Inside the open barn a thick-shouldered man in black pants, blue shirt, and a straw hat was doing something to the hoof of a horse. He was facing my direction, and had to have seen me drive up, but he gave no indication that he had. Between the barn and the house I could see Rebecca Zook. She was hanging sheets on a clothesline, her back to me. Either she didn't hear my BMW, or more likely, she'd been trained to turn a deaf ear to the world, confronting it only when absolutely necessary.

The children were a different story. They allowed their ball to roll down into Dead Man's Curve, and chased my car to the shade of a sugar maple. I parked and got out.

"Who are you?" The towheaded boy demanded in Pennsylvania Dutch. He was the smaller of the two boys, and because of his blond coloring, I assumed he was not of these Zooks. No doubt he was a neighbor child come to visit.

"My name is Magdalena Yoder," I said in English. "Who are you?"

The boy looked bewildered and turned to his dark companion.

"He does not yet speak the English," the older boy said, "but he is Zachias. My name is Elias."

"Good to meet you, Elias."

"I am eight years old. Zachias is only six years old. How many are you?"

"That's none of your business, dear."

Elias was undeterred. "Why do you come here?"

Elias spoke in a heavy German accent, a fact that did not surprise me. Like most Amish children his age, his only exposure to English would be school. There he would spend a total of eight years, taught by Amish teachers for whom English had also been virtually a second language, and whose education had also been terminated in the eighth grade. As he grew older, and had more exposure to the world, his accent would improve, but without the influence of radio or television, he would most likely always speak in a way that outsiders would find quaint.

"I came to see Rebecca Zook. She is your sister, right?"

"Yah, she is my sister. Why do you want to see her?"

"Really, dear, this isn't any of your business."

He scratched his head. "Are you the mother of that English man?"

"I'm no one's mother, dear," I said, and then felt guilty for denying the furry babe asleep against my bosom. "And just which English man are you referring to?"

"Ach, that man who made my sister—what is the word?"

"Pregnant."

"Yah. Pregnant." He giggled.

The towhead said something in Pennsylvania Dutch that I didn't understand. I asked Elias to translate.

"Zachias wants to know if Rebecca will have a baby or a colt."

"What?"

"Papa called the English man *ass*. That means horse, yah?"

I glanced at his papa, whose attention was no longer

on the horse, but on me. "Same genus, different species," I said flippantly.

The Zook boy nodded solemnly. "I hope it's a colt. Papa said I could have my own when I am this big." He held his hand about a foot above his head.

"That's nice, dear." I tried to move past them, but Zachias had another probing question.

"He wants to know," the Zook boy said, "if Santa Claus is real."

The Amish celebrate the birth of Jesus, but ignore entirely the cult of the fat, bearded elf. Still, their children cannot help but be familiar with the character. Every time an Amish family goes to town in the months of November and December, their senses are assaulted by Santa and his sleigh. Santa's sleigh, incidentally (along with his beard), has provoked many an Amish child to ask if the jolly bearer of gifts is in fact of their own faith.

"No, Santa Claus is just a story," I said.

"But he was here. Zachias and I saw him."

"When did you see him?"

"Today."

"I'm afraid that's impossible, dear. It's July. You don't see any snow for the sleigh, do you?"

"Ach, no."

"And did he have a red suit and a big bag of toys?"

"No, but he had a white beard and was fat."

"Well, dear, no offense intended, but that describes a dozen Amish men I know."

"Yah, but this man had a top beard."

"A mustache?" The Zook boy was extremely perceptive for his years.

"Yah, a mustache. And he spoke English."

During the seventeenth century, mustaches were in

vogue among European soldiers, and the pacifist Amish came to equate hair on the upper lip with the willingness to commit violence. Today, while virtually every adult Amish male sports a full beard, mustaches remain forbidden.

"Well, he wasn't Santa Claus."

I started walking toward Barbara but Elias stepped boldly in front of me. "Then who was he?"

"I don't know, dear." Strictly speaking that was the truth. I did, however, have a hunch.

"Elias! Zachias! Leave the English woman alone!"

The boys abandoned me and ran down the drive to retrieve their ball. Rebecca's father was striding toward me at a curiously un-Amish gait. In the meantime Rebecca seemed to have disappeared, perhaps behind a flapping sheet. Even *Grossmudder* had gone inside. I stood my ground.

"Miss Yoder, yah?"

"Yah—I mean, yes."

"Miss Yoder, you will leave now, please."

"But I came to see Rebecca."

He shook his head. "That will not be possible."

"Why not?"

"She is not here."

"Of course she is. She's hanging laundry."

"There is no one hanging laundry."

"Maybe not now, but there was a minute ago. Look, dear, you know as well as I do that lying is a sin."

"Ach!"

"I'll only take a few minutes of her time. And given her condition, she could use a rest, right?"

"Rebecca does not want to speak to you."

"Says who? Says you? Look, she's an adult. Doesn't she get to make up her own mind?"

"I am her papa." That said it all. Had Rebecca been sixty-five, unmarried, and living at home, she would still be obliged to obey her parents.

"Very well. Maybe you can at least tell me if a Dr. Bauer has been by today."

He said nothing, but his eyes had the look of a spooked horse.

"Ah, so he has been here."

"Miss Yoder, please leave. Now."

"Just one more question, if you will."

But Rebecca's father had lost his patience. He didn't strike me—that would have been unfathomable—or even push me. Instead, he acted as if I were no longer there.

"Elias," he called. "Zachias. Bring the ball up to the house. There is work for you to do inside."

Without another word he returned to the barn.

I may be pushy, and sometimes rude, but I am not mean-spirited. I might well have been able to barge into the house, or if Rebecca had been hiding among the flapping sheets, confront her there. To my credit, I held my head high, and climbing into my red BMW, drove calmly away. Only after exiting Dead Man's Curve, while on a rare straightaway, did I press the pedal to the metal. I mean, what good is it to have a brother-in-law for police chief, if one can't take a few liberties with the law?

"Dang," I said to Little Freni. "Dang."

Little Freni purred her sympathy.

When I was quite through venting and had slowed to the legal limit, I tried to make sense of the day's events. Dr. Pierce, by all accounts a good man, lay dead in Bedford's morgue. Dr. Bauer, on the other hand, had made a house call to the Zook farm. Some-how that didn't seem to be his style. Still, it was a considerate thing to do—*if* he thought Rebecca would need his services shortly. But if kindness was his motive, why did Rebecca's father seem so upset?

"Sweetie," I said to Little Freni, "you wouldn't mind terribly if we made a little detour, would you? The store doesn't close until five, and I have that can of tuna in my purse."

My pussy didn't object, so I made a left on Schlabach Lane instead of continuing straight into Hernia. A right on Kurtz Street and a left on Troyer, and we were at the hospital before you could say "rubber baby buggy bumpers" five times—well, at least say it correctly five times.

In the hospital parking lot I put Little Freni on the passenger side front floor, opened the can of tuna, and let her chow down. The fish was packed in water, but that mite of a kitten ate every last bite and licked the can clean. When she was through with her supper she looked like a furry baseball with add-on appendages. Sort of a Mr. Potato kitten.

A loud wail alerted me to the fact that she needed to use the parking lot, but once that was over she was quite content to crawl back inside my bra and settle down. By the time I reached the hospital door, she was fast asleep.

Now, I may have feet the size of continents, but I have been known to sneak up on people at times. Just ask Freni. Those are *her* hairs stuck to the plaster of my kitchen ceiling. But getting past Nurse Dudley is another matter altogether. That woman has the ears of a bat, and if the rumors I spread about her are true, had a seismograph surgically implanted in her buttocks. On cat's feet or not, fog couldn't sneak past her.

"Yoder!" she bellowed, without even looking up from her paperwork. "Get out of my hospital!"

I kept walking. "This isn't *your* hospital, dear. Besides, it's visiting hours."

"So?" My nursing nemesis looked like she'd been sucking lemon juice through a rhubarb straw.

"So, I have a legitimate reason to be here."

Nurse Dudley was on her feet and headed my way. "Ha! We don't have a psycho ward. Not yet, at any rate."

"Very funny, dear." I walked faster.

Nurse Dudley changed tactics and headed for the corridor door. She is a big woman, even larger than Mama was. With her hands on her hips, the woman's elbows touched both doorjambs.

"Ha, you can't get past me."

"Is Dr. Luther here?" Thank heavens I had suddenly remembered the director's desire to get Gabe on the staff.

Dudley's face darkened. "So, you're going to go whining to him, are you?"

"I'll whine him and dine him. Whatever it takes. Now, get out of the way."

"You think you're such hot stuff," she hissed.

Much to my horror, Little Freni hissed back.

"What was *that*?" Dudley demanded.

"That's just delayed sibilance. It tends to echo."

"You really are nuts, you know that?"

"Takes one to know one, dear." I cupped my hands to my mouth. "Dr. Luther, are you there? Dr. Luther?"

Nurse Dudley's arms dropped to her sides, but she didn't vacate the doorway. She merely turned, so that

in passing I had to brush against her enormous bosom.
Little Freni hissed again.

"Thibilance," I thaid, and squeezed past.

I found Jonathan sitting in an armchair next to Barbara's bed, an infant in his arms. Barbara was sitting
up in bed, nursing the other baby. Had it not been
for the kitten in my bra, I would have been in-
tensely jealous.

"Well, well, such a happy family," I said with forced
cheer. Forcing cheer is an acquired ability, at which I
have become rather skilled.

Both Jonathan and Barbara beamed. "Yah, very
happy," they said in unison.

"But two sets of diapers. That's going to be a lot
of work." I chuckled pleasantly. "Too bad they can't
use a litter box."

Barbara frowned. "Ach, a child is never too much
work. It is a gift from God."

Her attitude surprised me. The woman is normally
placid and easygoing. Motherhood, it appeared, did
strange things to one.

"Well, a gift, yes, but instead of one that keeps
giving and giving, this one never stops taking. You'll
be ninety years old and still worrying about these
two." At least that's what Mama used to tell me.
"Now a cat, well, fifteen years—twenty tops—that
sucker will be dead."

Little Freni yowled in protest.

"What was *that*?" Barbara was clearly alarmed.

"Nothing, dear. Maybe my stomach." As long as
you remember to say "maybe," it's not a real lie. Still,
it was time to change the subject. "Jonathan, dear,
how's your father?"

Jonathan shrugged.

"He has not left my side," Barbara said. The pride in her voice was unbecoming in an Amish woman.

"How very sweet, dear. Well, from what I've heard, Mose seems to be doing just fine. Freni calls now and then from the hospital in Bedford. I'm surprised she hasn't called here."

Barbara and Jonathan exchanged knowing glances.

"Come on, dears, you can say it. I won't breathe a word to anyone." Kittens obviously didn't count.

Barbara looked lovingly at her suckling baby. "Ach, it is just Nurse Dudley is so—so—"

"So mean?"

"Yah. I was saying to Jonathan that maybe his mama called, but we were not told."

"Nurse *Dead*ly," I said, "appears to hold a grudge against all of mankind." For the first time I noticed a Band-Aid on Jonathan's forehead. "She didn't do that, did she?"

Jonathan grinned. "Ach, no. That is from when I fell."

"He fainted," Barbara said. She giggled. Call me sentimental, but there is something particularly sweet about a six-foot-tall, two-hundred-pound giggler holding a nursing infant.

"You *fainted*?"

Jonathan blushed. "Ach, I was only out for a few minutes. I did not miss anything."

"When was this?"

"During the delivery," Barbara said. She giggled again.

My heart raced. "Oh, my heavens," I fairly shrieked. "This may explain everything!"

Twenty-seven

"**W**hat's all the commotion?" Nurse Dudley's enormous noggin protruded through the door space like a mounted lion's head.

"It's nothing, dear. We're just having a family celebration."

"Keep it down," she snarled. "This is a hospital, not a zoo."

"Yes, sir!"

Nurse Dudley glared at me with amber eyes. "One of these days, Yoder. One of these days." Then off she strode, no doubt to find lesser prey for her supper.

"Ach," Barbara said, shaking her head, "I will have to pray for that woman."

"Pray that she gets a job offer overseas. Now, dears, tell me again about this fainting incident."

"It was nothing," Jonathan said quickly.

Barbara smiled. "Yah, but it was a surprise. Jonathan has delivered many calves on the farm. Foals too. Sometimes he has to reach inside and turn them around."

"And that was the first time for fainting," Jonathan said.

I nodded encouragingly. "Well, I hear it's much different if the mother-to-be in question is your wife. So, at exactly which point did this happen?"

Jonathan squirmed. "Please, Magdalena, is this necessary?"

"That depends, dear. You see, if you were out long enough, it is *possible* your mama was right."

"Ach, but—but—I was only out a few minutes."

I turned to Barbara. "Can you confirm that?"

"It seemed like hours to me." She grinned.

I grinned back. Perhaps not unknowingly, but conspiratorially, nonetheless.

"But of course it wasn't, because you had one of the fastest deliveries on record. Still, it seemed like quite a while, did it? That Jonathan was out cold, I mean."

"Yah, but frankly, Magdalena, it is not so clear anymore."

"What's not clear?"

"I remember the pain, yah? And the joy, that too. But the memories are mixed up. It seems like—well, in a way it seems like it happened a long time ago."

"But that was only yesterday!"

"Yah, and in some way it seems like it happened just a few minutes ago." She yawned. "Ach, suddenly I am very tired."

"So, you're saying you're not a reliable witness?"

"Yah." She yawned again.

"Don't poop out on me now!" I wailed. "How about you, Jonathan? You didn't happen to look at your watch, did you? Maybe just before, and then again, after you kissed the floor?"

"Ach, Magdalena, I don't wear a watch."

Of course. No Amish person in good standing would wear such a worldly ornament.

"Well, was there a clock in the delivery room? Maybe you glanced at it!"

Jonathan had stood, still cradling little Jonathan. "My Barbara needs to take a nap." He nodded in his wife's direction. "Will you take Little Mose back to the nursery with me?"

I sighed. "It would be my pleasure."

I gingerly took the newborn from his mother's arms. Unlike kittens, small babies seldom land on their feet. At any rate, you can be sure I took great care not to drop him, and held him somewhat away from my scrawny chest. But even with the latter precaution, Little Freni was not pleased. She hissed like a leaky pot on a hot stove.

"Shhh," I said, repeatedly masking the hisses.

Barbara and Jonathan gave me odd looks but said nothing. Perhaps they thought my behavior was typical of English spinsters holding babies. But just for the record, despite all the hissing and shushing, or maybe because of it, by the time the four of us reached the nursery, Little Mose was fast asleep.

Nurse Hemingway rolled her eyes when she saw me. "Oh, it's you."

"Yes, it's me," I said. I tried to hand her Little Mose, but she took a step back, as if we might be contagious.

"You can put him there in the bassinet. The one on the left. He no longer needs the incubator."

I did as I was told. "Say, Hemmy, you wouldn't be free for a cup of coffee would you? I mean, you get a break, right?"

She glanced at an enormous watch with an orange face and a bright pink band. It looked entirely unprofessional. There was obviously not a drop of Amish blood in her veins.

"Actually, I don't get a break for another two hours. And then it's supper."

"Well, I could come back. Or, I tell you what—why don't you come by my place for supper?" I would probably have to cook it, but Nurse Hemingway was clearly not a woman of discerning taste. I didn't see my homemade victuals as a problem.

"Oh, I couldn't do that," she said, and took Little Jonathan from his namesake.

"Why not? I run an inn. I have guests all the time. Come on, it will be fun."

She looked like the raccoon I surprised in my grain silo, and I'm not just talking about her makeup either. "Miss Yoder, I didn't want to say this flat out, but I don't like you."

"What?" I hardly knew the woman, but for some reason that hurt me to the core.

"Please don't make me say it again."

I jiggled a pinkie in my right ear. "Perhaps I misunderstood you. I thought you said you didn't like me."

"There's nothing wrong with your hearing."

"But I'm a barrel of laughs! Aren't I, Jonathan?"

Jonathan looked like a doe caught in my headlights. "Well—"

"Oh, go on, and tell her, dear. Everybody likes me, right?"

"Ach!"

"Well, I never!"

"But I like you," he said, almost shyly. "And my Barbara likes you."

"And your mama!"

"Ach, yah!"

Nurse Hemingway flashed me a triumphant little smile. "Well, I don't like you. You're so pushy and rude."

"But I'm not!" I wailed. I turned to Jonathan. "Am I?"

"You see?" Nurse Hemingway crowed. "That's exactly what I mean. You push people into corners and you don't give them an 'out.' "

"That's not true. You just don't understand our ways because you're from Pittsburgh."

"Have it your way—*of course*." She turned her back. "Well, if you'll excuse me, I have work to do."

Humiliated, I said good-bye to Jonathan and left.

After leaving the nursery I pretended to need the ladies' room, and then after waiting a few minutes, I doubled back. Nurse Hemingway was still on duty, alone with the infants. Apparently she didn't have bat ears like Miss Dudley.

"Well, you don't have to swear," I said when she was quite through.

"What do you expect me to do when you scare me half to death? Dance with joy? Look, Miss Yoder, it isn't going to work. Nagging is not going to make me like you."

"Don't flatter yourself, dear. I didn't come back because of that—although I still don't agree with you. I came back because I have a few questions to ask."

She bent over and started to undo Little Jonathan's diaper that, incidentally, sorely needed it. I could smell it from the door. At any rate, as she lowered her head a lock of bleached blond hair fell across her face.

"Dang," she said. Only it was a lot worse than that. I gasped. "I'm telling! It's one thing to swear at me,

but you were looking right at the baby. What if he
grows up to be a Presbyterian? Or worse yet, a
Roman Catholic?"

She straightened. "Well, it's your fault. You've got
me really worked up." She smiled unexpectedly.
"Look, there's some rubber bands on that little desk
in the corner. Bring me one, will you?"

"I thought you were from Pittsburgh."

"I am."

"But you said—"

"Bring me a dang rubber band," she snapped. "Is
that too much to ask?"

I got the rubber band. "Pittsburgh born and
raised?"

She caught the stray strand with the rubber band
and secured it under her white cap. "Look, Miss
Yoder, I don't have time to bond. I've got a job to
do here."

"But you're not from Pittsburgh, are you? Pittsbur-
ghers call them gum bands, not rubber bands. It's one
of their foibles that makes them so delightful."

"Okay, so I'm not from Pittsburgh, what of it?"

"So, you lied."

"Big deal. I only did it to be accepted. You people
are so cliquish."

"Where *are* you from, dear?"

"New Jersey. You have a problem with that?"

I took a step back. Things were starting to fit
together.

"There *were* three babies, weren't there?"

"Don't be ridiculous."

"I'm not. I'm deadly serious."

"Look, I don't have time to argue nonsense. But
here are the facts. There were four of us present in

the delivery room, babies not included, and all four of us can testify there were only these two. These cute, adorable little twins." She made goo-goo sounds at Little Jonathan. There were two reasons now for me to gag.

I backed up another step and almost knocked over Little Mose's bassinet. "Sure, there were four adults in the room, but only three besides you. I just talked to Barbara and Jonathan. Barbara admits that she was not the most reliable witness, and Jonathan confessed that he flat out fainted, which leaves—"

"He said that?"

"Yes, he's certain of it."

Now it was she who backed away. "He was only out for a few seconds."

"Says you, dear. But I'm beginning to think he may have been unconscious a lot longer than that. Say, long enough for you or that gnome of a doctor to spirit away the third Hostetler baby."

"That's absurd." She was edging back toward the desk. No doubt she planned to call security. Well, let her. There is safety in numbers.

"And speaking of the dinky doc with a potbelly," I said, thinking aloud, "I don't think I trust him as far as I could throw him. Probably even less than that. If he's diabetic like he claims, why did I catch him pigging out on pancakes and those phony fruity syrups?"

"You did?"

She was grappling for the phone behind her. "Well, there could be a number of explanations for that. Maybe the syrup was that sugarless kind or—" She paused.

"Or what? Because Wanda Hemphopple wouldn't

know sugarless from a hole in her beehive. Fat-free either. That's what makes the food there so good."

"Maybe this will help explain things," she said. In her right hand a pistol gleamed.

Twenty-eight

"**O**kay, big mouth, any more questions?"

"Uh-uh, mind if I sit down?" It was a legitimate question. My knees were knocking like the cylinders on Papa's old Edsel the year Susannah put sand in the gas tank.

"Actually, I do mind. You're taking a walk with me."

I braced myself on Little Mose's bassinet. "And if I refuse?"

"Then I shoot."

"But there are babies in here for crying out loud!"

"Oh, don't worry, I'm a very good shot. My ex was a cop. He taught me to shoot on a civilian range. I can sign my name on a target. It's a lot more fun than just making bull's-eyes."

That took care of my urge to duck behind a bassinet. "You won't get away with this, you know. Nurse Dudley has ears like a bat. Pop me off and she'll be back here in a flash."

Nurse Hemingway laughed. "Good. I hate the woman. And there are plenty of bullets in this thing."

"Any silver bullets?"

She smiled grudgingly. "Don't bother to kiss up; I

don't like you any better. Now put both hands behind your head and move to the door. Quickly!"

I did as I was told. As I started for the door, hands on head, I noticed for the first time that the nursery blinds had been drawn. Had they been that way from the beginning? Or had she used that special control at her desk? It didn't matter in any case. As soon as I stepped into the hall, I'd make a run for it. Good shot or not, she would have a lot harder time hitting me out there. Without the babies to worry about, I could zigzag like a chicken drunk on sour mash. And if I could make it to another room, I could lock the door, or jam it with a piece of furniture. I may be skinny, but I'm strong.

"Hold it right there," she barked, just before I reached the door.

I was still in the room, and a ricocheting bullet could have put an end to one of Freni's two remaining grandbabies. I had no choice but to obey.

Like a lamb led to the slaughter, I stood there and waited to die. It is true what they say: my life, pitiful as it was, flashed before my eyes. A childhood of taunts for being too tall, a critical, overbearing mama, a somewhat wimpy papa, a selfish sister, a bogus marriage to a man who I thought adored me, but who then betrayed me, and did I mention sex? And not just with the washing machine either, but with the aforementioned love of my life?

I suppose a more virtuous Magdalena would have felt regret for all the folks she'd wronged, for all the paths not taken, but alas, as I stood there, waiting to take that bullet to the back of my head, all I could think of was that what I had come to take for granted with the Maytag, I had missed out on experiencing with Aaron.

"Don't move, or I'll blow your head off," Nurse Hemingway growled, in what I now clearly heard as a strong New Jersey accent. A second later she jammed a hypodermic needle through my clothing and into my derriere.

I have vague memories of staggering around, stepping into unfamiliar clothes, and climbing into a strange car. I think I may have sung a little. Hymns, I think. "Bringing in the Sheaves" comes to mind. So does "Ninety-nine Barrels of Beer on the Wall." Go figure.

At any rate, at some point I fell into a deep sleep. When I awoke it was dark, my heart was pounding, and my mouth felt like the Sahara in a dust storm. My wrists were shackled in handcuffs, and I was seeing double. Through the ringing in my ears I could hear Nurse Hemingway's jarring accent.

"Don't worry, I already gave you the antidote. You're going to live."

I struggled to speak, but my tongue flopped about in my mouth like a freshly caught perch in the bottom of a rowboat.

"It's tubocurarine chloride," she said. "It's used in surgery as a muscle relaxant. That pathetic hospital in Hernia didn't have any—hell, they didn't even have an operating room—but that didn't stop me. I carry my own with me. In my line of work you never know when it will come in handy."

The fish flopped about in the boat some more.

"What do I do? Ha! I thought you had that all figured out. I steal babies, that's what I do."

"Thyew *thwat*?"

"I babynap. Newborns only—that's my specialty. There's a big market for that. Especially white Anglo-Saxon babies, whose parents are unlikely to have had much exposure to drugs or AIDS. You Mennonites and Amish make perfect pickings."

"Thyew do this by yourthelf?" The fish in my mouth had been replaced by a tongue, albeit one that was not very obedient.

"Don't be ridiculous. This is a two-person operation. I move into a territory, scope it out, and then, if I find potential targets, I send for Doc. You might be surprised how many small towns are hurting for doctors. No questions asked. And if it's an itty-bitty dump like the one you have in Hernia—geez, what an appropriate name, Doc has no trouble getting me on staff. Anyway, after we've skimmed what we can from the baby crop, we move on to the next burg."

I was aware that we were indeed moving. It was dark outside the car, and still difficult for me to focus, but from the landscape that streaked by the windows and the occasional blurry sign, I determined that we were somewhere on the Pennsylvania Turnpike.

"How do you thkim off babith?"

"That's the hard part, and that's where I earn my share. You have to have a real feel for that. Sort of a third sense. Unwed mothers are usually a good bet. And religious fanatics. You wouldn't believe how many stool pigeons have given their babies to the Lord."

"*What?* You mean the angel Levi Gindlesperger met at the Sausage Barn was really Dr. Bauer?" I don't mean to sound prejudiced, but those folks at the First and Only True Church of the One and Only

Living God of the Tabernacle of Supreme Holiness and Healing and Keeper of the Consecrated Righteousness of the Eternal Flame of Jehovah needed help in visualizing their heavenly hosts. I thought Gabe the babe was an angel when I first met him, but he had pects, not a paunch.

Nurse Hemingway laughed wickedly. "How stupid can you get!"

"Apparently pretty stupid, dear, because you're going to be spending a whole lot of time behind bars." It was an effort to move my head, but I did. "And what's more," I said, looking at her double image, "you wouldn't look good in stripes."

"Shut up!"

Of course I didn't. "But ten thousand dollars! You were going to give the Gindlespergers ten grand, right? Speaking purely as a businesswoman, that seems a bit generous. How did you expect to make a profit?"

"Ha! That just shows how little you know about *this* business. I can get as much as seventy-five for a healthy baby boy."

"Seventy-five *thousand*?"

"That's for the whole package. Fake birth certificate included. For girls it's usually less. Fifty maybe, sixty tops if both parents have blue eyes and blond hair. For boys it's the other way around. Dark hair brings in more. It's that whole dark and handsome thing I guess."

"That's outrageous!"

"Tell me about it."

"Girls should be worth as much as boys!"

All four of Nurse Hemingway's shoulders shrugged.

"Hey, I don't make the rules. It's what the market can bear."

I fumed for a few minutes. The steam coming from my ears clouded the car windows, but it did my eyes some good. Gradually the two Nurse Hemingways melded into one. Thank heavens there was less of that bleached blond hair to look at.

"But Freni's grandbaby—Barbara and Jonathan's baby—is it a boy?"

"A girl. But both parents have light hair, and the mother has blue eyes. Besides, we really had no choice. The juice I gave Mr. Hostetler to drink didn't kick in until the third baby was born. He'd already seen the two boys. I'm telling you, that man is built like an ox."

"You spiked his punch?"

"So to speak."

"Because he wouldn't sell his children?"

"We never asked him. As you can see, there was no need. Multiple birth situations where the fetuses are healthy and close to full term are fairly easy pickings. Especially when the parents are uneducated."

I saw a sign for Breezewood, Pennsylvania. We were headed east, toward New Jersey.

"The Hostetlers may not be educated, dear, but they're not stupid."

"Whatever. But it was you who caught on, not them."

"Apparently Dr. Pierce caught on as well."

"He was kind of cute, don't you think—if you like older men?"

"I couldn't tell if he was cute or not, dear. Blood is unbecoming."

"Maybe you won't feel so sorry for him, if I tell you he was in on it from the beginning."

"Dr. Pierce was your third partner?"

"Nah, he was too straight for that kind of thing. But he sold us his patients' files. No questions asked, that was the deal."

"Why would he do that?"

"It seems he had a cash flow problem. He was recently divorced, you see. Apparently she took him to the cleaners. He was about to lose that fancy-schmancy house. Drove him to drink. Anyway, the damn bastard had a conscience and—"

"Don't you swear in front of me!"

"Ha! What are you going to do about it?"

I struggled stupidly against the cuffs. "Well, maybe I can't do anything, but God can."

"Ha, that's a laugh."

I gave her the evil eye on the Lord's behalf. "I'd be careful, dear, if I were you. Back in seventh grade Mabel Bontrager took His name in vain and—ach!" I could see what should have been my reflection in the driver's side window. But instead of my comely visage staring back at me, I beheld the horrified face of an Amish woman. An Amish woman with a long horse face and a nose that had its own zip code.

Twenty-nine

I stared at the apparition in the window.

The evil nurse chortled. "Oh, so you're just now noticing? I've got you all done up to look like an Amish woman. Bet your friends wouldn't recognize you now."

My arms felt like rubber, but with a great deal of effort—during which Nurse Hemingway had a good laugh—I managed to pull down the passenger side mirror. Someone's black travel bonnet had been clamped over my own white prayer cup. I looked down at my dress. Why hadn't I noticed? I was wearing a dark blue dress with wrist-length sleeves, and over that a black pinafore. But where were my own clothes? *And Little Freni?*

I reared back, craned my neck, and peered into the neckline of the Amish dress. Fortunately the previous wearer had possessed a far fuller bust, and the neckline of the frock gaped. You can imagine my relief when I not only espied my own dress under the Amish garb, but the fuzzy head of my sleeping pussy.

"Whew!" I was stupid enough to say it aloud.

Nurse Hemingway laughed. "Don't flatter yourself. I'm not into women. I didn't undress you, if that's what you're thinking. Fortunately for you, Mrs. Hostetler is a bigger woman. And she was pregnant, of course. Her clothes slipped right over yours."

I snapped the mirror flap closed. "I don't know what your game is, toots, but it isn't going to work."

"Well, it's working fine at the moment, and that's all that counts. I lived in that hellhole Hernia long enough to learn a few things about the Amish." She pronounced it *Aye*-mish, a fact that grated on my nerves like nails on a chalkboard. "And one of the things—"

"Oh, is that a fact, because—"

She rudely cut me off midsentence. "I've learned that although Amish are forbidden to own and drive cars, they may ride in cars owned and operated by we lowly *English*. So, you see, Magdalena Portulaca Yoder, if anyone noticed us leaving town, they certainly didn't see *you* sitting beside me. And when I've moved your meddling butt far enough so that you wouldn't be recognized, even without any clothes, it's curtain time."

"Move me across the state line and it's kidnapping," I wailed, and then remembered my stolen niece. "Where's the baby? Where's Barbara and Jonathan's little girl."

"That's for me to know, and for you to never find out."

My heart dropped into my stomach and bounced several times. "She's *not*—I mean, you *didn't*—you *couldn't* have!"

"There you go being ridiculous again. Like I said, she's worth a cool sixty grand, and I've got a customer all lined up. No, that little sweetie is on her way right now to a pair of loving arms."

"Just one pair? She had two pairs of loving arms

right where she was. Dozens more, if you include extended family. You won't get away with this, you know. Sooner or later you're going to get caught, and then either you'll fry like a flank steak, or you'll end up in jail, for life, with a boyfriend named Jill. And seeing as how you're so stupid, I say it's going to be sooner rather than later."

"Shut up."

Breezewood zipped by in a streak of lights. The mountains pressed in again, the landscape now just shades of darkness. A few pinpricks of light marked the hamlet of Burnt Cabins, and then we plunged into total darkness.

"The Tuscarora Tunnel," I said. "One of the longest in America."

She said nothing.

"Say, what do you call five blondes standing in a row? You give up? A wind tunnel!"

"Shut up!" This time there were a few additional words that I can't repeat, and the sound of the back of her hand striking my cheek. There was also the taste of blood in my mouth from where I bit my tongue. This time literally.

Yes, I can be foolish at times—sometimes even downright stupid, but I'm not completely untrainable. I swallowed my blood and kept my big mouth shut. Meanwhile, I prayed for deliverance.

Believe it or not, prayer calmed me, and I was half dozing when I felt us veer off the highway. I jerked awake. My heart, which had resumed its rightful place in my chest, was now pounding at a million beats per minute.

I can't adequately describe my relief when I saw that we had pulled into a service area of the turnpike system. I know that my sigh was heard in Hernia—Gabe later confirmed it—and I may have lost some bladder control. But just a little. At any rate, that somewhat homely building with its neon signs advertising food and gas looked as good as anything the Pearly Gates might have to offer.

"Thank you, Jesus."

"You can thank Him in person later," Nurse Hemingway said with a cackle. "This is just a pit stop. For *me,* not you. Try anything—*anything*—and that baby ends up in a Hoboken Dumpster."

I gasped. "You wouldn't do that! She's worth a lot of money to you. You said that yourself."

"Just try me and see." She ripped the key from the ignition, slammed the door behind her, and took off at a run.

"Well, when you gotta go, you gotta go," I said to Little Ferni. Already I'd learned the biggest blessing any pet bestows on its owner: the right to talk with impunity when no one else is around. A conversation between myself and a mirror might be grounds for committal, but prattling to my pussy merely made me eccentric.

Please understand the dilemma I was in. I mean, there was nothing to stop me from getting out of the car and making a run for it, except my concern for a baby that I had never seen, and who may, or may not, have been alive at that moment. I honestly believe I would have remained in the car, awaiting my certain death, had not the most remarkable thing happened. Truly, it was a miracle.

Hardly a minute had passed since Nurse Hemingway's bleached tresses disappeared into the service center, when I saw a couple exit from the building and head in my general direction. This, I knew, was no coincidence, but an out-and-out answer to my fervent prayers. The Good Lord has sent someone to save me! Perhaps they were angels—their faces were in silhouette, but already I could tell that they were more attractive than Dr. Bauer. And vaguely familiar. I leaned forward, peering intently through the windshield that was fast fogging up.

"What a beautiful night," the female angel said, and I recognized her voice.

"Thank you, Lord!" This time I shouted. "Thank you for answering my prayers!"

Then, without waiting for a "you're welcome," I finagled the door open and lunged outside. Then I plunged, right to the pavement.

I have never been drunk, not even so-called tipsy, but I have had the flu upon occasion, and once I had a middle ear infection. Therefore I am familiar with the phenomenon of rubbery legs and no sense of balance, but nothing like this had ever happened. I literally kissed the ground. However, I managed to take the brunt of the fall on my right shoulder, and thus spared the life of my child. Little Freni barely stirred.

The Redigers, bless their heavenly Mennonite hearts, ran to my rescue. "Miss Yoder, is that you? Are you all right?"

"I'm fine as frog's hair," I rasped, spitting out granules of weathered pavement.

Donald helped me to my feet. "You're wearing handcuffs!"

"What?" Gloria took a closer look. Her eyes widened, and I knew what she was thinking.

"It has nothing to do with sex!" I wailed. "I've been kidnapped."

"Kidnapped?" they echoed.

"This bleached blond bimbo babynapper, who also happens to be a nurse, nabbed me in the nursery."

They shook their heads in confusion.

"I can explain everything, but there isn't time now. Listen, you've got to help me."

Donald still had a steadying hand on my shoulder. "Of course. We'll get you inside. There are phones in there. We can call the police."

"No!" I twisted painfully to get the service building door in my line of vision. "She's sadistic! She's threatened to kill Freni's granddaughter if I cause any trouble. What I need you to do is to write down the license plate number of this car and call the police. Tell them there's—oh, my gosh!"

Gloria grabbed one of my shackled arms. "What is it?"

"It's Dr. Bauer! Her evil accomplice."

"Quick," Donald said. "Our car is this way, we'll think of something."

"But I can't leave! And if he sees—"

"Too late. He's headed right this way."

"Oh, Lord," I wailed, "what am I going to do?" That wasn't just an expression mind you. I was praying again.

Gloria tugged on my arm. She seemed almost as panicked as I. "You won't be of any help to the baby at all if you're dead—if we're *all* dead!"

It was perhaps unforgivable on my part, but I fled with the Redigers. Since Dr. Bauer had seen me talking to others, the ax had already fallen. The only hope the Hostetler baby had at all was if I survived to tell the police and the F.B.I. everything. You understand, don't you? I mean, at least there was a *chance* to save the child if I spilled my guts to the authorities. If I spilled my guts on the pavement—well, then, no one benefited.

The Redigers were parked only three spaces away, but we barely made it. Dr. Bauer was running toward us like a crazed gnome and shooting! Shooting! Right there in the middle of a service-area parking lot. Bullets were zinging past our ears and ricocheting off the pavement and surrounding cars like out-of-control fireworks. Think of it as the Fourth of July, but without the Roman candles.

Thank heavens the dinky doc was such a lousy shot. All three of us managed to get into the Redigers' car without being hit. Their car wasn't hit either, or if it was, no serious damage had been done. It started immediately, and by the way Donald drove, you would never guess he had even as much as a drop of Mennonite blood. I don't know how many Gs the car was capable of doing, but it produced at least one.

"Geeeeeee!" I said as we careered out of the lot on two wheels, going the wrong way, and then jumped the median while simultaneously making a U-turn, much like those teenage boys I'd see on skateboards in Bedford.

Once on the turnpike, however, he melded smoothly into the traffic and drove at the prevailing speed. Both Donald and Gloria seemed remarkably calm, almost as if nothing had happened. No doubt they were folk of greater faith than I. Those Indiana Mennonites have always seemed to me to be a stronger strain than we here in the east. No doubt it's those prairie winds that toughen them up.

"It's best not to draw attention to ourselves," Gloria

said. "We could be pulled over by a state trooper and ticketed."

"Yes, but isn't that what we want?"

She turned in the front seat to face me, and in the light of a passing car I could see that she was wearing lipstick. Lipstick! And not just a pale pink either, but harlot red. How had I missed that before? Maybe those Hoosier Mennonites were emotionally strong, but at least one of them was spiritually challenged.

"I don't think we should be putting our faith in the world, do you?" she asked.

"What?"

"Perhaps that wicked little man already called the police and fed them some lies. If no one believes us, and we end up in jail, how is that going to help that sweet little baby? No, I think we should keep driving until we can take refuge with some people I know we can trust."

"Like *who*? Oprah Winfrey?" I've never seen her on TV, but she's stayed twice at my inn. I'd trust that woman with my life, wouldn't you?

Donald laughed. "Gloria has a cousin up the road."

"How far up the road?"

"Just a little ways," she said. "Maybe half an hour. You'll be all right until then, won't you?"

I grunted. "I hope your cousin is a locksmith. These handcuffs are starting to chafe."

"Maybe if you just close your eyes and try to relax," Donald said. He had a soothing voice, and would have made a good radio announcer.

Frankly, a little shut-eye might do me good. The gunfire in the parking lot had sent my adrenaline soaring. Without that surge, I very much doubt if I would have been able to reach the Redigers' car, even with their assistance. But now, safely in the backseat of their car, I felt the adrenaline drain from me like water from an unplugged bath. I leaned back against the seat. It was soft, cool leather.

Why not just stretch across the backseat and take a little nap? I was safe now, in the capable, if somewhat naive hands of the Indiana Mennonites. Perhaps sleep would do me some good—at least it would take my mind off the handcuffs. Yes, sleep, my body screamed. Sleep, sleep!

I often fight my body's urges, but this one did not involve breaking any of the Ten Commandants, or even the so-called Seven Deadly Sins. After all, it was dark out, and thus quite permissible to sleep. Cautioning myself not to enjoy the experience too much, I closed my eyes and allowed myself the luxury of sliding sideways along the soft leather seat. My right cheek came to rest on the buttery cushion, but it wasn't as comfortable as I'd imagined.

"What on earth?" I opened my eyes and sat up.

There, lying on the seat, was a binky. You know, a baby's pacifier. I picked it up with shackled hands.

"Anything wrong?" Donald asked.

"I didn't know you had a baby."

"We don't."

"Well, somebody does, because here's a pacifier."

"It's a rental car," Gloria said. "That must have belonged to the previous user."

"Yeah, probably." But in the light of an encroaching automobile I saw a package of disposable diapers. It had been shoved halfway under Gloria's seat. For a few seconds I was even able to read the print. *Newborns to three months.* "Which company did you rent this from, because—"

I heard the click of the safety being released before I saw the gun. I'm no expert, but the pistol Gloria was holding looked remarkably similar to the one belonging to Nurse Hemingway.

Thirty

Great Granny Yoder's Toad Stroganoff

✦

(Heart-smart and ahead of its day)

1 pound ground turkey
½ cup chopped onion
½ cup sliced fresh mushrooms
8 ounces linguine
1 can diced tomatoes

Brown and crumble meat in large fry pan. Add onion, mushrooms, and tomatoes and cook over slow-to-medium heat. Cook linguine according to package directions to al dente. Add to other ingredients and simmer until heated through.

Serve with green salad and crusty rolls. Serves four normal people, or one Yoder.

Thirty-one

"**C**uriosity killed the cat," Gloria snarled. "And now it's going to kill you."

I was stunned. It's one thing for a Mennonite to slip a little and paint her lips, but this was almost beyond comprehension.

"This is a joke, right?"

"Shut up."

"*What?* Donald, dear, tell your wife this isn't funny."

"You're damn right," Donald said. "It isn't funny. Now shut up like she says."

Telling a living, breathing Yoder to shut up is like telling the Mississippi to flow backward. In the words of Susannah, "It ain't gonna happen."

"You guys aren't Mennonites, are you?" I asked, as the possibilities began sorting themselves out.

"We never said we were."

"But you are both so clean-cut—well, Donald, you are at any rate. Your wife used to be, until she dolled herself up to look like the whore of Babylon. I thought sure you were Mennonites."

The gun wavered. With all due respect to my home state, the Pennsylvania Turnpike has more than its fair share of potholes.

"Well, you thought wrong," Gloria snapped. "Now shut up."

"Certainly, dear." I managed to keep my lips zipped for several seconds. "Wait, a minute. You guys aren't part of that babynapping ring—oh, my gosh, you are, aren't you?"

The scarlet lips parted and pursed. "Bingo."

"But you helped save me from that dinky doc and that ditzy blonde."

"That ditzy blonde," Gloria growled, "is me."

"Give me a break, dear. That was a bottle job, if I've ever seen one. Her roots were dark as sin. Your hair, on the other hand, is a rather attractive shade of brown. A little bit darker than mine maybe, but nice all the same."

Gloria's free hand reached up and whipped off a wig. I gasped. "Get out of town!"

"Do you know how hard it is to find a wig with braids? Damn things's hot," she grunted and tossed it over her shoulder. It landed on the seat beside me, looking for all the world like a tailless muskrat.

"It *is* you!"

Gloria laughed maniacally. "You didn't really think I was a dumb Mennonite, did you?"

I figured I was already on that train—so to speak—bound for Glory, so what did I have to lose? One may as well die talking.

"Yes, I did think you were a Mennonite, but then again, I'm famous for jumping to conclusions. I often trip myself up that way. Speaking of tripping, did you hear about the blonde who tripped over her cordless phone?"

"Huh?"

"It's supposed to be a joke," Donald said. I could

see only one corner of his mouth in the rearview mirror. He was definitely grinning.

"That same blonde studied for a blood test," I said, "and failed."

She thrust her gunhand closer to me. "Oh, I get it, these are blonde jokes."

"Of course, they don't really apply to you," I said quickly, "seeing as how you're a fake blonde and everything."

"Don't you ever shut up?"

"Not if I can help it, dear."

"This will help you," she said, and undid her seat belt. The next thing I knew the cold barrel of the pistol was pressed against my forehead. "One more word out of you and I'll blow your _____ head off." There is simply no need to shock you with her choice of adjectives.

"She means business," Donald said quietly.

I prayed like I'd never prayed before. I prayed for what some may think to be the biggest miracle of them all; I prayed that the Good Lord would keep my big mouth shut. Yes, I know, God shut the lions' mouths on Daniel's behalf, but a Yoder mouth is even a taller order.

My prayers were heard. Although I wanted to ask Nurse Hemingway, or whatever her *real* name was, if she'd heard the one about the blonde who spent twenty minutes staring at an orange juice carton because it said "concentrate," I couldn't as much as move my lips. In fact, I became downright fearful that I was paralyzed. I even tried communicating *that* with my eyes, but I couldn't get them to roll.

It occurred to me that perhaps the Almighty had turned me into a chunk of salt—like Lot's wife—just to protect me from myself. This was an exciting, if somewhat disconcerting thought. What if the Good Lord forgot to desalinize me when the threat of danger had passed? While I firmly believe that my soul will return to my Maker, and have no qualms about my earthly body pushing up daisies—at the *appropriate* time—it had never occurred to me that I might end up in somebody's water softener. Or worse yet, sprinkled on sidewalks to melt snow.

At least my ears still worked. "She's scared stiff," Gloria chortled, before finally turning away.

Maybe that was it. I prayed that it was. I prayed that when the time was right, I'd get full use of my faculties back. And if that was not to be, if I really was a chunk of salt, I asked that I might be broken down into smaller pieces, like kosher salt, and used in an ice cream churn. An *electric* ice cream churn. I'd always wanted one of those, but for some reason, I've never gotten around to springing for one. Well, if I got out of this scrape alive, I was going to make a trip into Pittsburgh and buy the finest electric ice cream maker on the market. *And* I was going to buy a size twenty shift and proceed to eat so much of my home-made ice cream that I filled out the dress. I'd make vanilla, of course, and strawberry, and in peach season . . .

I discovered I was licking my lips, and they weren't the least bit salty. I tried moving my tongue, quietly, and within the confines of my mouth. It seemed to work quite well. Meanwhile, Donald and Gloria had involved themselves in a nasty argument.

"I say we pull over at the next picnic area and kill her." Gloria had a somewhat nasal voice and it was beginning to get on my nerves. How I could have pegged her for Hoosier is beyond me.

Donald, however, still sounded Midwestern. "Then what?"

"Then we toss her in the woods. Look at all these damn trees. Have you ever seen so many in your life?"

Donald thumped the steering wheel with the ball of his left hand. "It's night. We don't know how deep these woods go. There could be a house anywhere. Someone might see us."

"If there were houses, there would be lights," Gloria snapped. "What do *you* suggest we do, lug her all the way back to New Jersey? Maybe put cement boots on her and throw her into the Hudson?"

"Actually, I was thinking of the Delaware River. Or better yet, since we'll be cutting up on 81, why not take her up to the top of Delaware Water Gap, and throw her off? I bet lots of people have fallen there. Even jumped."

"Yeah? Well, why would someone jump from a cliff high enough to kill them?"

Even I knew the answer to that. No doubt if you gave Nurse Hemingway a penny for her intelligence, you'd get back change.

Donald didn't answer his wife's question. Instead he pointed to a sign.

"Town coming up. I *told* you."

"Well, we could have killed her back there. I'm beginning to think you're chicken."

"The hell I am!"

"Buc-buc-brack!" The imitation blonde did a horrible imitation of a chicken.

"Bitch!"

That, believe it or not, was one of the nicer names

they called each other. It went downhill from there.
They used words I've never even heard of, and I
thought Aaron had taught me everything there was to
know about the mindless world of profanity. Folks
who swear do so because they lack the wit to express
themselves. Of that I'm sure.

At any rate, the couple in the front seat got so
caught up in their childish fight that I was forced to
face the window, lest they see the smile plastered
across my face. We were now passing through the city
of Carlisle, and on a rather well-lit stretch of the turnpike, and that's how I happened to notice the little
girl in the car next to us. She was staring at me. No
doubt she found my Amish getup fascinating.

I stared back.

She waved.

Then it occurred to me that perhaps *she* was the
answer to my prayers. "Help!" I mouthed.

She stuck out her tongue.

"Help! Get the police!"

The girl was a lousy lip-reader. She stuck two fingers
in either side of her mouth and made a horrible gri-
macing face.

"They're babynappers! They're going to kill me.
Help!"

I mouthed my words carefully, but she still didn't
get the point. She stuck her entire fist in her mouth
and crossed her eyes. In the meantime the car she was
in started to pull ahead.

In foolish desperation I slid my shackled hands over
the seat and retrieved the binky. To my surprise, and
hers, I popped the pacifier in my mouth. At this point
Donald and Gloria were practically coming to blows,

and my action, bold as it was, went mercifully unnoticed by them.

The little girl laughed and pointed at me. Then she poked her mother in the front seat. The mother turned, at first obviously annoyed, and then amused.

I spit the binky out. "Help!" I mouthed again. "Help! Call the police!"

Thank heavens her mother was a better lip-reader.

Thirty-two

"**A**nd that's where I come in, right?" Susannah had taken a huge bite of freshly churned peach ice cream and it oozed from the corners of her mouth as she spoke.

"Take it away!" I cried. "It's all yours." I'd been trying to stifle my sister for the last fifteen minutes by keeping her mouth full, but of course to no avail. It had merely been a waste of ice cream. She is a Yoder after all, and nothing but a pistol could tie her tongue.

"So you see," Susannah said, "if it hadn't been for me, when the little girl's parents called the police, they might have dismissed it as a prank call."

"Ach, what did I miss?" Freni had been changing a diaper during the first part of the story, and apparently Little Mose was adept at what baby boys do best. When Freni returned from the bedroom she was still wiping her face.

"You must have missed the most important part," Susannah said, ignoring my glare. "It was me who got the A.P.B. out on Mags's kidnapping."

Freni blinked behind bottle-thick glasses. "A.P.B.?"

"All points bulletin. Of course Melvin actually called it in, but it was me who noticed that nose."

I tried to cover my proboscis with one hand. It took two.

"Can we skip that part?" I whined.

"But it's the best part." Susannah turned to her audience for confirmation. Besides Freni and me, the audience included Barbara, Jonathan, and Gabe. We were, incidentally, sitting on the front porch of the Hostetler homestead. It was the first day home for all *three* babies, and now with Little Mose changed and dry, it looked as if all three were finally asleep.

"Yah, it was a good part," Jonathan said.

Barbara nodded her agreement.

I glared at each in turn. "Go on," I wailed to Susannah, "but don't exaggerate."

Susannah rolled her eyes. "*Please,* I don't have to. So anyway, after I discovered Dr. Pierce's body, Mags dropped me off at the Material Girl, that fabric store in Bedford. And guess what? They gave me a job."

"How much does it pay?" Barbara asked. From what I could gather, Freni was even more interfering as a grandmother than she was as a mother-in-law.

"It's just minimum wage," Susannah said with surprising patience, "but I can buy from the bolt at half off."

Barbara nodded. "These little ones will need lots of clothes."

"Right. Now where was I? Oh, yeah—so I don't have a ride home, you see, and it must have been a bad hair day or something, because I wasn't getting any offers. So I was standing by the road when Naughty Eddy got off work. He owns a hair salon right next door to Material Girl. Anyway, Naughty Eddy offered me a ride, and of course I accepted. He isn't really that naughty, you know. I mean, it's all a bluff. He says it's because of a war injury, but I heard he was born that way, with only—"

"Ach!" Freni squawked. "The nose! Tell us about the nose."

"Okay, okay, but don't rush me. So, we were coming down Route 96, and we're almost to Hernia, when we pass this car coming the other way. I happen to look over and there's Mags, sitting in the backseat, all decked out like an Amish woman. Man, did I do a double take."

"How did you know it was her?" Freni asked. If you ask me, it was not an innocent question.

"Because of the nose!" everyone chorused.

"Very funny," I humphed. "Lots of Amish women have big noses."

"I think it's a great nose," Gabe said. "Noble even."

Susannah smirked. "No offense, sis, but none of the Amish women have noses so big they require their own zip code."

Everyone laughed, Gabe included.

"Anyway, I made Naughty Eddy turn around and pass you guys so I could get a better look, and sure enough it was you. I waved and honked, but you were sleeping or something."

"I was *unconscious,* dear."

"Yeah, whatever. So then we turned around and went back to Hernia, and Naughty Eddy dropped me off—boy, did Melvin blow a gasket when he saw him. It took me forever to calm him down, but then after he'd rolled over and gone to sleep, I got to thinking about Mags again. She does a lot of weird stuff, but I've never seen her dress like an Amish woman before—except for that one time in Ohio, when she had to, and that was just to save her life.

"So I called the PennDutch and this crabby English woman answers and says that Mags isn't there, and her dreamy boyfriend doesn't know where she is either"—Susannah looked meaningfully at Gabe—"and that's when I started thinking that something was wrong in a major way. So, I woke Melvin up, and made him issue the A.P.B. He didn't want to at first, but I made him."

"And how did you do that?" Gabe winked at me.

"We don't want to know," I said. "The point is the Carlisle police caught up with us—only by then we'd left the city limits, so they notified the sheriff. After a two-county car chase, the Redigers—and believe it or not, that is their real name—were apprehended, and yours truly survived basically unharmed. Well, except for the ten years that wild ride took off my life."

Freni nodded solemnly. "Yah, you look older."

"But not ten years, sis," Susannah said loyally. "More like five."

"That was just an expression, dear," I said to Freni. "I think I look pretty good considering everything I went through, if I must say so myself."

That was a hint, if ever I've given one. Unfortunately, Gabe allowed the opportunity to pass him by.

"That Dr. Bauer just ticks me off," he said. "A bad apple like that can really besmirch the name of the entire medical community."

"Yah, I hear he was a drug dealer," Jonathan said in hushed tones.

"From Colombia," Barbara said.

It was time to step in with some facts. "He wasn't a dealer, dears. He was a user. A heroin addict. I should have known when I caught him drowning his pancakes in syrup. Anyway, that service area was supposed to be a rendezvous, but they got into an argument and Dr. Bauer went berserk and started shooting. The cops got him right away. But like I said, I should have known when I saw the syrup that he was no diabetic."

"You can't keep track of everything," Gabe said kindly. "And this was a slick bunch of characters. Renting that apartment next to your sister *and* a room at PennDutch—now that was a stroke of genius."

Sometimes it is I who cannot leave well enough alone. "Yes, but I should have known that Nurse Hemingway and Gloria Rediger were one and the same person. They both reminded me of someone, and besides, I had a pair of twins staying right there at the inn who showed me what a huge difference a hairstyle can make."

Gabe eased his long lean legs off his rocker, sauntered over to me, and took my ice cream bowl gently out of my hands. Then much to Freni's amusement— and Susannah's envy—he refilled it. The ice cream, incidentally, had been churned in an old-time crank machine. I still had not been to Pittsburgh to pick up my electric version, or my size twenty dress.

"But all's well that ends right, right?" He chuckled.

Despite the cold bowl, my fingers burned where his had touched me. "Right. I'm just glad Donald broke down and told the sheriff everything."

"Yah, and now we have our baby back," Freni said. She was still patting her face with her apron.

"And three other babies," I reminded her. The Redigers and Dr. Bauer were not the only members of the New Jersey-based babynapping ring in the area. Donald ratted out a pair of cohorts in Bedford who ran a baby "clearinghouse." Baby Hostetler was among the four newborns discovered there. Thanks heavens all four infants were in good health.

"Baby this, baby that," Susannah said, rolling her eyes. "You still haven't chosen a name for her, have you?"

Freni's eyes glistened. "Of course."

Jonathan rose and put a hand tenderly on his mother's shoulder. "Yah, Mama, but it isn"t what you think."

"What do you mean?"

Barbara looked directly at me, and I could tell she was purposefully avoiding her mother-in-law.

"Mama, we owe so much to Magdalena—"

"Yah?"

Jonathan swallowed hard. "Mama, Barbara and I agree that we should name our little girl Magdalena."

Freni swayed, and without Jonathan's restraining hand, might well have fallen off her rocker. *"Magdalena?"* she croaked.

"Yah, Mama. Magdalena Veronica Hostetler."

"Freni is the diminutive of Veronica," I said for Gabe's edification.

"Oh, Mags, that is so neat!" Susannah, with no thought to my full bowl of ice cream, threw herself into my arms.

I should not have worried about spilled cream, not when I still had secrets to disclose. To everyone's astonishment, except for mine and Gabe's, my chest hissed at Susannah. To no one's astonishment, her bra barked back. My chest hissed again.

"Ach," Freni wailed, "and now she makes with these games!"

"To the contrary, dear." I dug deep and hauled out a blinking Siamese kitten.

Susannah backed up, knocking over the ice cream churn. "What the heck?"

"Look what I've got," I said, beaming. "You're not the only one who can lug a pet around in her lingerie."

Susannah righted the overturned churn. There was a new respect in her eyes.

"Oh, Mags, he's precious. Where did you get him?"

"It's a she, dear, and she's a present from Gabe."

"What's her name?"

"Little Freni," I said, and then clamped a hand over my mouth. I really wouldn't hurt my friend for all the world.

And although she'll deny it until the cows come home, Big Freni smiled.

I said good night to Gabe on the front porch. It is in clear view of Hertzler Road and thus eliminates a lot of temptation. Besides, all we did was talk. I asked Gabe if he wanted to affiliate with Hernia Hospital— as a consultant only—but he firmly refused. He didn't have time, he said, to write the great novel *and* heal broken hearts. Unless that heart was mine, I thought, but wisely kept my mouth shut.

Inside the empty inn, I took stock of the remainder of the week's events. The Moregold twins had made remarkable comebacks when they learned I would not be waiting on them hand and foot. When they left for Disney World, courtesy of Yours Truly, we were on good terms. Not so the vamp Vivian and her boy-toy Sandy. They bailed out the night of my capture, and without paying the balance of their bill. But I had her credit card imprint, and besides, to be perfectly honest, I hadn't been the best of hostesses.

As for the mystery guest in Room 6, well, that was a riddle still waiting to be solved. I'd pushed a note under his door that very morning, telling him to vacate. I had a full contingent of guests scheduled to arrive the next day.

"Well, shall we go up and see if he's gone?" I asked Little Freni.

She meowed in agreement.

We took the elevator up. There is no point in risking my neck needlessly on those impossibly steep stairs. Not when there is no one around to come to my aid.

The door to Room 6 was ajar, and it appeared to be empty, but I knocked anyway. "Hello? Hello?"

There was no answer.

I stepped inside. "What a mess," I clucked. "Just look at that, will you? Dirty plates all over the place, half-eaten food—somebody's going to pay to clean this up." I picked up one of Mama's Sunday dishes. "Yuck, what is this stuff? Fried peanut butter and banana sandwiches?"

Little Freni plaintively asked to be let down. I set her gently on the bed.

"Don't eat any of this stuff, dear," I warned. "It's liable to make you sick."

Little Freni ignored me, sniffed one of the plates, and gave it a cautious lick. Then she literally turned up her nose and bounced away. Something else had caught her attention.

"What on earth is that?" I demanded. Little Freni was batting at something, some kind of a wire. I picked up the shiny object. "Why, it's just a broken guitar string," I said.

I gave it back to Little Freni who purred.

Thirty-three

Homemade Peach Ice Cream

✦

(For crank-type freezer)

1 cup sugar
½ teaspoon salt
6 egg yolks
2 cups whole milk
2 cups heavy cream
½ teaspoon vanilla
1 pint peach pulp, or four ripe peaches,
  peeled and mashed

Mix sugar, salt, and egg yolks. Slowly add milk. Cook in top of double boiler until bubbles appear around edge of pot. Allow to cool before adding cream, vanilla, and fruit.

Pour mixture into freezer can. Replace dasher, cover can, and adjust crank. Place can in tub. Fill freezer one-third full of ice. Add layer of salt, and then ice, alternating until full. Use six parts ice to one part rock salt. Turn crank until it becomes difficult. Pour off meltwater. Remove lid and pack mixture down in can. Repack with ice and salt and allow to sit for two hours.

P.S. No babies, either real or imaginary, were harmed during the writing of this book.

SIGNET

The First John Darnell Mystery

THE CASE OF CABIN 13
Sam McCarver

The year is 1912, John Darnell is a professional investigator whose specialty is debunking theories of paranormal activities. He is approached by the managing director of White Star Trans-Atlantic Oceanliners with a proposition. A bizarre series of suicides on board their newest ship, the Titanic, has the employees whispering of ghosts and violent spirits. Darnell agrees to look into the matter, and once on board, he tallies up a list of very-much-alive suspects, each with their own sinister motive. But when the fate of the Titanic is sealed in the icy waters of the Atlantic, will the killer get away with yet another murder?

___ 0-451-19690-2/$5.99